***"You shaved your beard,"* Molly murmured, surprise and regret in her voice.**

Rand put both hands on her shoulders and searched her eyes. "You really liked it?" he asked incredulously.

"Yes, it was . . ." She had to grope for the word. "Romantic," she blurted out, then added, "You looked like what you are."

"Ah-h-h," he said, understanding at last. "Correction. I looked like what *you* think I am."

When she didn't answer he touched her cheek with his fingertips. The small caress sent a warm shiver down her spine. "A Viking earl? Is that how you see me?"

She swallowed and nodded.

"If that's what you want . . ." His arm slid around her waist, pulling her slowing against him. The hand at her face raked into her hair to hold her head steady while his descended.

His deliberately slow movements certainly gave her plenty of warning, Molly thought fleetingly, and wondered why she had no intention of heeding it. . . .

WHAT ARE *LOVESWEPT* ROMANCES?

They are stories of true romance and touching emotion. We believe those two very important ingredients are constants in our highly sensual and very believable stories in the *LOVESWEPT* line. Our goal is to give you, the reader, stories of consistently high quality that may sometimes make you laugh, sometimes make you cry, but are always fresh and creative and contain many delightful surprises within their pages.

Most romance fans read an enormous number of books. Those they truly love, they keep. Others may be traded with friends and soon forgotten. We hope that each *LOVESWEPT* romance will be a treasure—a "keeper." We will always try to publish

*LOVE STORIES YOU'LL NEVER FORGET
BY AUTHORS YOU'LL ALWAYS REMEMBER*

The Editors

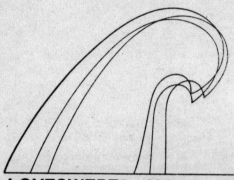

LOVESWEPT® • 134
Marion Smith Collins
Out of the Clear Blue

BANTAM BOOKS
TORONTO • NEW YORK • LONDON • SYDNEY • AUCKLAND

OUT OF THE CLEAR BLUE

A Bantam Book / March 1986

LOVESWEPT® and the wave device are registered trademarks of Bantam Books, Inc. Registered in U.S. Patent and Trademark Office and elsewhere.

All rights reserved.
Copyright © 1986 by Marion Smith Collins.
This book may not be reproduced in whole or in part, by mimeograph or any other means, without permission.
For information address: Bantam Books, Inc.

ISBN 0-553-21747-X

Published simultaneously in the United States and Canada

Bantam Books are published by Bantam Books, Inc. Its trademark, consisting of the words "Bantam Books" and the portrayal of a rooster, is Registered in U.S. Patent and Trademark Office and in other countries. Marca Registrada. Bantam Books, Inc., 666 Fifth Avenue, New York, New York 10103.

PRINTED IN THE UNITED STATES OF AMERICA

O 0 9 8 7 6 5 4 3 2 1

Dedicated with love to:

Rita Angel Spitzli, a friend of more years than either of us wants to remember;

Mary and Chuck Bullard, who made my last visit to Tidewater so memorable;

And to all the wonderful people in the Tidewater Area of Virginia, especially these whom I feel privileged to call friends: Rebecca, Sharon, Elaine, Paula, Susan, Brenda, Pat, Teresa, July, Judy, Jo, Leslie, Lesley, Lodeen, Rosemary, Irene, Tracy, Mary.

Melissa Wall at the Daily Press, John Willis and Cindy Wheeler at WVEC-TV:

One

The crowd was sparse at the ceremony this year, Molly Beddingfield thought when she arrived, and decided it was because of the weather. Winter had decided that the last week in March was a good time to deliver a vicious reminder to the residents of Virginia Beach that it, like one of nearby Norfolk's more famous sons, would return. The unkind season never liked to give way to the soft southern spring.

Molly parked her three-year-old compact in the Holiday Inn lot above Twenty-fifth Street and sat for a moment looking down on the group of people huddled in coats and mufflers. The clouds were so dark and low that it might have been evening, rather than two o'clock in the afternoon.

The angry wind blowing directly off the turbulent Atlantic redoubled its efforts to scatter the papers on the speaker's podium. The distinguished man who was standing in front of the microphone made a grab for one, and missed. It sailed over his head and landed smack in the face of a tuba player.

As she watched from the warmth of her car, Molly wondered with a shudder if the weather in Moss, Norway, where at this moment a sister ceremony was taking place, could be any worse. Resigned to the fact that some unspeakable part of her anatomy was going to freeze, she sighed, got out of the car, and closed the door with a gentle bang, not wanting to disturb the speaker.

As though it just had been waiting for another victim, the chilling wind picked up her long auburn hair and swirled it around her head, into her eyes and her mouth. Blindly she snatched a woolen cap from her pocket and pulled it down over her ears, tucking wayward strands of hair up under the cuff. She buttoned her red reefer to her neck and hid her bare hands in its flannel-lined pockets. Ready as she would ever be, she descended the steps to street level and edged in behind the forty or so diehards gathered there. She knew it was her own fault. If she'd been early she could have been among all those lovely warm bodies instead of huddled here on the edge.

She only half-listened to the words of the speaker, allowing her thoughts instead to drift across the sea to the group on the other side. She hoped they weren't as cold as she was.

The wind made yet another pass at her, whipping her pleated plaid skirt around her thighs. Sheer hose was no protection for her legs. She touched her nose to confirm its presence, then jammed her hand back into the comparatively warm haven of her pocket.

The master of ceremonies finally proclaimed the end of the speeches. Molly breathed a sigh of relief, which was only slightly tinged with guilt, because she usually enjoyed the annual ceremony. It appealed to the romantic in her. An active and fanciful imagination could take her into the past as easily as her extensive knowledge of the history of this memorial could. She had cut her teeth on the moving tale. . . .

That day, in March of 1891, must have been just as cold and blustery as this one, but worse. The rain, which today was only a promise, had been falling in thick, wind-driven sheets, obscuring vision.

A Norwegian bark, the *Dictator*, one of the tall three-masted sailing ships whose history so enthralled Molly, was floundering off the coast of Tidewater, Virginia. The SeaTack Lifesaving Station #2 at Virginia Beach had been alerted to the ship's peril and was preparing for a valiant rescue attempt that would be only partly successful. Molly's great-grandmother, a guest at the resort hotel, had been a witness to it all and an active participant.

Molly couldn't see over the heads of the people in front of her, but she knew what was happening. While the two national anthems, the United States' and Norway's, were being played, a delegation would carry a wreath from the memorial site to the edge of the ocean, a hundred yards away. The strongest of them would hurl the flowers as far as possible into the water and hope, in vain, that it wouldn't be washed back up on the shore, until nightfall, anyway.

Her hair was the first thing about her that caught

his attention. As she got out of the car the wind tossed it about her head as if it were a vivid streamer, and even this colorless day couldn't dull its lively vibrance. He felt a moment's regret when she tugged on a knitted cap.

He watched as she made her way gracefully, on the light feet of a dancer, down the steps from the parking lot to the street. She wore very high-heeled shoes, and her legs, visible only from the knee down, were bare and slim and startlingly beautiful.

She crossed the tarmac to the edge of the crowd. He straightened his shoulders, which had been hunched against the cold. Over the heads of the people between them, his eyes followed her progress. Then, as though he were being drawn by some unexplained, invisible force, he began to work his way around the crowd for a closer look.

Molly suddenly realized that she was no longer cold. Someone had moved up behind her, standing very close to cut off the biting drive of the wind. She twisted her head to look over her shoulder.

What began as a grateful smile faded into an expression of absolute astonishment.

Unable to believe her eyes, she whipped her head back to the front. It couldn't be! she thought. Her fanciful, romantic nature had been packed away after college, along with the Princeton banners and the ribbons from football chrysanthemums. This was unreal. She caught her lower lip between her teeth and stared for a long moment at the flowers on the hat of the woman in front of her. Nonsense, she told herself. It was her imagination, fostered, no doubt, by the occasion.

Tentatively she ventured another look over her shoulder . . . at the man who had filled her childhood dreams with extravagant flights of fantasy, the man pictured in storybooks as handsome pirate, an adventurer, a daring sailor. He might have been Eric The Red . . . in person.

This Eric, however, was flesh and blood, radiating energy and potent virility, standing resolutely against the brutality of the wind as though it were a weak breeze. He was more, so much more, than her dreams . . . and bigger!

The man behind her gazed over her head. In fact, he gazed over everyone's head. He was at least six feet four, and his shoulders, under the navy worsted overcoat, seemed to stretch forever. A shiny billed hat shaded his forehead, and she caught a glimpse of gold braid under the white cover.

"Brawny, bearded warrior of the sea." The quotation popped into Molly's mind just as the warrior's eyes dropped to meet hers, and her knees threatened to buckle. They were the clearest, bluest eyes she'd ever seen, framed with lines that told of visions over distant horizons. His face was rugged and tanned, wide-browed and strong-boned. A flash of white teeth split the thick blazing-red moustache and the full beard, which was just a shade too well trimmed, too civilized for the image.

His smile was absolutely devastating, and she returned it dizzily. He was certainly one of the romantic heroes of the sea, who had sailed down through the centuries to this time, this place. To her.

Dimension and space were suspended. Half-turned to face him, Molly stood still, returning the stranger's gaze with an incredulous expression. *I have waited all my life for you*, she thought.

He seemed to be caught in the same absorbing trance. His blue eyes prowled slowly over her upturned face, touching down like a caress on her arched brows, her blue-gray eyes, with their thick hedge of lashes, her small nose, and wind-stung cheeks. At last they settled on her mouth with a hungry look, stealing her breath. That was when she turned to face him fully.

She felt as though the two of them were encased in a bubble of enchantment, sealed off from the rest of the scene. External sounds and sights faded away, leaving in Molly only an overwhelming awareness of this man. Her heart thundered in her ears; her breath quickened under the stranger's darkening gaze.

After a time, which might have been measured in minutes or hours, he stretched out a hand. Moving as though she were in a dream, Molly withdrew hers from her pocket and gave it to him. His gloved fingers curved slowly inward until his grasp was firm and unrelenting. To Molly's whimsy it was a symbolic gesture. Her hero from the sea had come to claim her.

When he finally spoke, Molly, still in the spell of reverie, almost expected the unintelligible language of the Vikings. "What?" she murmured.

"Shall we move inside?" he repeated without a trace of amusement.

The bubble was broken. That deep, low voice was definitely New England, she thought with a sharp pang of disappointment. The realization that she had been staring at him as though he were the reincarnation of some Norse god sent vivid color up to stain her cheeks. She withdrew her hand from his grasp and looked around at the dispersing crowd. "I'm s-sorry," she stammered. "It's just that you're so . . ." Her wide eyes returned to him and her voice trailed off.

"That settles it," the stranger said firmly, giving her another glimpse of his appealing smile. "Tomorrow it goes!"

She shook her head, not understanding, and not yet completely free of the confusing daze. "What goes?"

"The beard." He ran his gloved hand over his chin. She could hear the rasp of leather against the springy hair. "If it scares away lovely women . . ."

"Oh, no," she denied quickly. "It's very nice."

"Then let's go inside and you can tell me why you look so shocked," he suggested smoothly. "The ceremony is over."

Shocked? thought Molly. He didn't know the half of it.

There were only a few stragglers left on the street. Everyone else had disappeared into the adjacent motel for the reception that followed the ceremony. Molly had planned to skip the reception and hurry back to work. When the stranger took her arm, though, she realized she had no intention of protesting. They circled the statue of the "Norwegian Lady," which was the focus of the memorial.

The man paused, and looked up at the nine-foot statue, the replica of a ship's figurehead, clad in the vest and flowing dress of Norwegian tradition. "She's a majestic sight, isn't she?" he said.

"Yes, magnificent," Molly whispered, but she was looking at the man, not the comely and buxom woman. The words on the plaque at the base of the statue found their way from somewhere deep within her memory to her lips. " 'I am the Norwegian Lady. I stand here as my sister before me to wish all men of the sea safe return home,' " she recited softly.

The wind snatched at her words, but he heard. His eyes locked with hers. A half-smile curved his mouth. "Home. That's a very comforting sentiment." He spoke the words with simple sincerity, but there was a wealth of meaning in the way he looked at her.

For years the site had been a featured landmark for civic activities in Virginia Beach. But at that moment the setting belonged only to them. Something elemental in the wild wind, blowing sand, and turbulent water was theirs alone, a rendezvous where a woman's heart was first touched and warmed by a man of the sea.

The artificial heat hit them like a blast furnace as they entered the motel. Molly unbuttoned her jacket, and the stranger took it from her, hanging it beside his overcoat on a hook inside the door.

He was wearing the dress blue uniform of a United States Navy officer. The pristine white shirt was in startling contrast to his deep tan. Over the left breast pocket of his dark coat was row upon row of decorations and symbols that meant nothing to Molly. She skimmed over the evidence of his worldliness, but identified the two and a half stripes of gold braid that circled the sleeves just above his cuff as denoting the rank of lieutenant commander.

He had been studying her just as carefully. She knew her tailored outfit camouflaged her rather flamboyant figure, but when he'd finished his inventory she had the feeling he could recite her measurements with uncanny accuracy. "Aren't you going to take off your cap?" he asked. In the secluded hallway, the tone of his voice was more personal, as though they shared a special secret.

"What? Oh, yes." She tugged off the knitted wool toboggan. Her hair blazed free, tumbling in delightful disarray across the shoulders of her blazer and halfway down her back.

He caught his breath. "I think I should have read my horoscope this morning," he said softly. "Maybe I would have been better prepared for meeting a beautiful redhead."

Molly frowned. "My hair isn't red, it's auburn." Her reaction was mechanical, a reflex whenever anyone made reference to her hair. "*Yours* is red." Actually their hair was very close to the same color, a blend of russet and burnt umber. His might be slightly lighter, she decided from what she could see under his hat, the shade that Titian had captured so beautifully on canvas.

He took off the hat, confirming the truth of her observation, and set it on a shelf above their coats. "I apologize." His smile tilted in understanding.

She was caught again in the magnetic field of his gaze. "Apology accepted," she said quietly, smiling half to herself. "You probably get even more teasing than I do."

"Still, I imagine we'll set off a few sparks between us as we . . . get to know each other," he suggested in a tone suddenly heavy with innuendo. Holding her gaze effortlessly with his fathomless eyes, he added, "We are going to get to know each other, aren't we?"

He certainly did this well, Molly thought. He didn't touch her, didn't have to. With only the sexy rasp of his voice and the eloquence in his deep blue eyes, he cast a spell of sensuality that wrapped around her, igniting the sparks he spoke of.

A bark of laughter from the reception room brought Molly sharply back to her senses. In another minute she might very well have walked straight into the arms of a total stranger, she thought with shock. Outside, the encounter had been a romantic phenomenon; in this close space, it definitely descended to the level of the earthy. A man as handsome as this one would be as expert in the art of seduction as his suggestive remark indicated.

To Molly's great relief six generations of Tidewater breeding slowly, but inevitably, came to her rescue. She couldn't blame the man for his obvious assumption, not in the light of her equally obvious reaction to him. But now, for a reason she couldn't explain, it became imperative that she erase any idea he might have that she was vulnerable to his advances. She was in danger of being swamped by him, of drowning in that clear blue gaze, if she didn't pull herself together. A romantic daydream, spawned from a love of the sea when she was a teenager, was no excuse for losing her sense of perspective as an adult.

With a gigantic effort she first freed her gaze. Then her stubborn chin tilted to just the right angle. Straightening her shoulders, she managed to look down her nose at him, despite the fact that he was nearly a foot taller than she.

"Do you really think we'll get to know each other?" she asked in a voice that was totally at variance with her earlier soft tones, a voice that clearly stated he was dreaming if he thought such a thing.

Totally unaffected by her put-down, he planted his fists on his lean hips, threw back his head, and laughed, a rich, full sound of pure masculine mirth coming from deep within the broad chest. "How long did you have to practice to get that right?" he asked with an outrageous grin.

"Not long," Molly answered coolly. The chill in her voice was in direct contrast to the burning glow beneath the skin of her face.

His grin slowly faded as the stranger studied her for a long minute, but he didn't comment on the blush.

Thank goodness, Molly thought, relieved but totally vexed with herself. She hadn't blushed since she was fourteen. She didn't even know the man's name and he already had reduced her normally composed and confident demeanor to the level of adolescent stammering.

Seemingly unaffected by her attempt at withdrawal, he took her arm to lead her into the reception. "I'll find us a seat and get our coffee," he said. "You fill a plate for us. Be sure to get enough. I'm hungry."

Us? "I beg your . . ." Before she could take exception to his high-handedness, he had disappeared into the crowd. She gave an unladylike snort and turned in the opposite direction. Who had given that arrogant sailor a license to order her around?

The room set aside for the reception was filled. Colorful crossed flags of red, white, and blue, representing the United States and Norway, decorated round tables along the walls. A huge arrangement of red and white carnations and larger flags graced one end of the tea table. People milled about, laughing, talking, some still rubbing their hands together to restore their circulation.

Molly smiled and nodded to a few people she recognized, an automatic response. Her thoughts were taken up with the tall, romantic looking stranger and her most uncharacteristic response to him. She reached for a plate and began to fill it with the colorful array of foods from both countries. Who was he? she wondered. Cheese straws and pecan tarts joined dilled herring and gravlox until her plate was full. An officer in the U.S. Navy, she answered herself, who had wandered in on a ceremony that was a tradition in Virginia Beach. In weather like this? No one in his right mind would just wander in on such a day. A drop of sour-cream sauce spilled over the rim, and she absently transferred the plate to her other hand and licked her finger.

One of the ladies behind the table, a member of the auxiliary of the fire department, smiled at her and offered a tray. "Try one of Cornelia's bourbon balls, Molly. They're delicious."

Molly looked at her loaded plate in dismay. There was no room for another thing, not even one of the small delicacies. "I'll have to come back, Sissy," she said, returning the smile weakly.

What was she doing? she asked herself. She'd just had lunch. Suddenly she felt a stirring of what could only be described as panic. She was following the stranger's assertive instructions without the slightest question.

As a young girl she might have found it pleasant to fantasize about a domineering buccaneer sweeping into her life, issuing commands like ocean waves, one rolling over the next. But the reality of being ordered around—and following those orders—was scary as hell to an adult woman.

She turned from the table, to find the stranger at her elbow. "Here." She shoved the plate at him. "I have to go now. I hope you enjoy the reception."

He was a quick thinker, she would have to give him that. A reflex action would have dictated that he take the plate. But he avoided it and instead, with a warm palm at the small of her back, turned her smoothly in the direction of an empty table.

Short of dumping all the food on the floor, Molly was forced to retain her grip on the plate. She rolled her eyes and willed her spine *not* to turn to jelly, as it was predisposed to do under his touch. He held her chair for her, then settled his large, fit body onto the one beside her. Taking the plate from her nerveless fingers now—now, when it didn't help—he set it on the table between them.

She tried once more. "I have to get back to work," she said. Her boss, Admiral Jennings, had told her to take her time, but she didn't think his generosity would extend to her dallying with a stranger.

"The food looks good." he said, ignoring her protest. "Have some."

"No, thank you. I'm not hungry."

"Come on, Molly. I'll bet you've never had dilled herring." He speared the tiny fish on his fork and popped it into his mouth. "Um-m-m. That is delicious."

She looked at him in blank surprise. "As a matter of fact, I have it every time I come to this reception. How do you know my name?"

"I asked," he admitted with a grin. "Marjorie Beddingfield, called Molly, Assistant Director of the Maritime Museum, descended from the first settlers of Virginia Beach, twenty-four years old, spinster," he recited.

Molly stiffened. Her whole life, reduced to the bare essentials. It sounded so sterile, so bleak, when spread out like that, and she resented his pointing it out to her. She was happy, content with her simple lifestyle, and loved her career. Some day, when the Admiral retired, she was sure to be appointed director of the museum. True, the pay was terrible, and money always a problem. But that was so in any line of museum work, and she had already had a few articles published, which was the accepted way to supplement income.

Taking refuge in the custom and formality she knew well, she blocked the unease from her expression and shot the man a quelling glance. "The fact remains that we haven't been properly introduced," she said primly.

The fork halted abruptly on the way to his mouth. Slowly he lowered it to the plate and gave a silent whistle. "Maybe I should have said Victorian spinster," he murmured.

"Because I prefer courtesy and decorum?" she asked. "I realize that good manners are hopelessly out of date, but there are some of us who think it's a shame." Good Lord! she thought. She sounded like a prig.

The fact was that Molly was totally at a loss. This man flustered her as she'd never been flustered before, and the only crutch she had to lean upon was the crutch of convention, of correct behavior. Reared by circumstance in a family of gentlewomen, she was unprepared for the masculinity of this handsome giant. By choosing the career she had, she lived a large portion of her life in the world of yesterday, and it was brought home to her with sudden clarity how limited her experience really was.

She stared down at her hands, which were resting loosely in her lap, belying her inner agitation. How she would love to carry on the bright, careless conversation of a flirtation, but the simple truth was, she didn't know how. The men she dated, was used to, were ordinary men, pleasant, polite, not at all hard to talk to. They stirred only the most negligible sensual responses in her. This man was anything but ordinary, and the responses he stirred were awesome.

A large, warm hand covered her fingers. "Look at me."

Courage lifted her head and pride urged her to meet his gaze.

He seemed to sense the war going on inside her, and when he spoke, his voice was gentle. "Molly, when I first saw you . . . out there . . . with the wind in your hair, I felt something . . . almost a gut feeling that we'd known each other before. I didn't even know your name, but there was an awareness between us. I can't believe you didn't feel it too."

I did! she shouted silently, but she couldn't say that out loud. How would she express it? "I think you are all of my dreams come to life"? "I've been waiting for you forever"? She bit back a hysterical laugh. He'd think she was certifiably insane. At this moment she thought so herself.

He was studying her seriously, but there might have been an annoyed sparkle in his eyes. "Have I insulted you?" he asked finally.

"Oh, no!" She couldn't let him think that, but in the process of explaining she made a further mess of the conversation. "Not at all. I'm sorry if I gave that impression. I know I'm . . ." She tried to laugh off her stammer. "But you still haven't told me your name, and I—"

"Stay here," he interrupted, and got to his feet. "Don't move. I have a better idea."

He was gone only a moment. When he returned it was with the Norwegian consul from Norfolk in tow. "Jan," he said without preamble, "will you present me to this charming young lady?" His manner was as formal as her own, but there was a lingering sparkle in his eyes, and Molly wasn't sure if it was amusement or anger. "Please inform her that I am perfectly respectable."

The ambassador chuckled. "You'd have me perjure myself?" he teased.

"Jan, please."

There was a warning in the deep voice that didn't

escape Molly. How odd, she thought. She knew the ambassador very well, and he had never shown a teasing side to her before. She started to get to her feet in deference to his age and position.

"No, don't get up, Miss Beddingfield," he said. "How are you?" His smile was as charming as the half-bow.

"Fine, thank you, sir."

"May I present Rand Eriksson? He is substituting for his father this year, whom I believe you've met."

"Y-yes. Thank you, Mr. Ambassador," she said falteringly. Of course she knew Russ Eriksson! He was the son of Erik Eriksson, one of the surviving seamen from the *Dictator*. Her great-grandmother had pulled the young Erik, Rand Eriksson's grandfather, from the sea.

After the tragedy of the shipwreck, Erik Eriksson had remained in the United States and, through the years, the families had kept loosely in touch. Erik had moved to Massachusetts to begin a small shipbuilding business, and his son, Russ, was now one of the foremost marine architects in the world. Russ Eriksson and his wife, Joanna, usually dined with Molly's aunt when they were in town.

Now that she thought about it, Molly vaguely remembered their mentioning a son, but her memory didn't stretch to this red-haired giant. Rand must not ever have come to the ceremony with his parents, but then, she hadn't gone every year.

"Well, Rand is respectable. Not perfectly. You know what they say about sailors," the ambassador went on with a twinkle in his eye. "But I think you'd be safe in a crowd of people, anyway." He clapped the younger man on the back. "Give your parents my warmest regards, Rand."

"I will, sir. Thank you," said Rand, returning the handshake.

"Is your aunt here today, Miss Beddingfield?"

"No, sir. She delegated me to represent her because of the weather."

"Wise woman. I don't remember its ever having been so windy." The ambassador answered a hail from the next table with a wave, smiled at them, and moved off.

Rand sat down. "Is that proper enough for you?"

"You made me sound like a prude," Molly admonished in an undertone. Her fingers ranged nervously over the cutlery in front of her. Now that they'd been formally introduced, now that the barrier of protocol had been removed, she was still stiff and oddly at a loss with this man.

Rand hooked an arm over the back of his chair and looked at Molly speculatively. A beautiful woman who wasn't wearing any jewelry to indicate engagement or marriage didn't usually hold him at arm's length with such conventional conduct. It was an intriguing experience, especially after the scene on the beach. He couldn't have imagined her response to him out there. She had placed her hand in his as though she were making a gift of herself.

He frowned. And he had taken it as though he were accepting. The experience had been uncanny. "Look . . ." He leaned forward suddenly.

She jumped. It was an involuntary reaction, but she still jumped.

He shook his head. "You're unbelievable, lady. What century do you come from?"

Annoyed with herself, she let that annoyance spill over onto him. "The nineteenth, evidently," Molly snapped.

He laughed, but it was an odd laugh. "At least you admit it."

He was so close now that she could see the different flecks, gold and green, that deepened the blue of his eyes. Letting her own lashes fall to shield her expression, she shifted uncomfortably in her chair and lifted her cup to sip from it. "I hope your father isn't ill," she said. Her attempt to change the subject sounded stilted even to her own ears. "I can't remember his ever having missed this ceremony before."

Rand shrugged. "Not really ill, but his age makes travel difficult. I've just been transferred to Virginia. He deputized me to be here in his place."

"Please give him my regards, and your mother too."

Still watching her in that careful way, he nodded. "I will."

"We always enjoy seeing them. My aunt will be disappointed." Molly smiled her regret, feeling as if her lips were made of concrete. The tension across her shoulders was beginning to seep up into her neck. If she didn't get out of here soon, it would become a full-blown headache. "If you'll excuse me, I really do have to get back to work." She started to stand, but again his large hand stopped her.

His fingers curled around her shoulder, his touch gentle but firm. "Will you have dinner with me tonight, Miss Beddingfield?"

She hesitated. She would like to have dinner with

him, very much, she decided suddenly. She opened her mouth to accept, but before she could answer he spoke in exasperation as though to a backward child.

"I'll even engage a chaperone if it will make you more comfortable," he added sarcastically, letting his hand fall.

"Don't mock me!" He had misunderstood her hesitation, but that was no excuse for his remark. She felt her animosity build. "I may be a prude, Mr. Eriksson, and I may be Victorian in my attitude, compared to the women you're used to, but I am not unconscious. You have no right to be rude." What had she been thinking? she wondered. She didn't want to go anywhere with this—this sailor. "I have plans for tonight," she said, hating the haughtiness in her voice, but grateful for the shelter of her anger.

"Damn!" Rand ran an agitated hand through his thick hair and slumped in his chair, wondering why he was bothering with all this. Molly Beddingfield was definitely not his type of woman.

He tried to remember what his father had told him several years ago about the Beddingfield women—refined, ladylike, polished, lovely, et cetera. He'd dismissed his father's description as the idle, possibly wishful, observations of another generation, but obviously he'd been the one who was mistaken. He studied Molly's features, while admiring the composure that permitted the study.

She was pretty, her bone structure delicate, her every movement decidedly feminine, inspiring the most antiquated feelings of chivalry in him. He hadn't felt chivalrous in . . . Hell, he'd *never* felt chivalrous.

She stirred other, more disturbing and far more primitive feelings, too, that he was at a loss to explain. He experienced an unmistakable urge to lean forward and cover those tempting lips with his, to sweep her up into his arms like a hero in a B movie. He wanted to take her someplace private, someplace where he could awaken the sleeping sensuality he sensed was beneath the surface of her polite facade.

Her gorgeous body was all but hidden by the severity of her clothes. She should be in soft fabrics, misty colors, he decided. An unsought, unexpected mental picture of her in something sheer with ruffles, her hair spread out on a pillow, stirred his desire to a startling degree.

Still, it was a quality from within her that had first jolted him so thoroughly. From the moment he'd looked into those strange bluish-gray eyes he'd been affected. A sparkle, a spirited energy, radiated outward to catch and hold him, as though with sun-warmed chains. He'd found himself mesmerized, an unusual—no, a unique—reaction.

"Look, Molly," he said finally, with a sigh of irritation that was aimed more at himself than her. "Let's start over. I apologize for embarrassing you, for coming on too strong, for anything else you think I might have done." He shook his head again, not quite believing what he was saying, or that he was saying it so poorly. "This is crazy. At first I thought you were playing games, but, lady, you make the Puritans look like sons of Bacchus."

At Rand's words Molly took in a long breath, filling her lungs completely. "And you have a marvelous capacity for making an apology sound like an insult."

She rose. "Good-bye, Mr. Eriksson. Perhaps we'll see each other at next year's ceremony."

Rand stood, too, but slowly, taking his time. "Oh, we'll see each other long before that, Miss Beddingfield," he promised with an enigmatic smile. "I fully intend to show you the way into my century."

"Don't hold your breath. I won't be the woman in this port," Molly said sweetly, turning from him. She made her way through the crowd, acknowledging with hurried politeness the greetings of her aunt's friends. She grabbed her coat and hat off a hook by the entrance, but didn't bother to put them on. Escape was uppermost in her mind. She had made a drastic mistake when she'd thought of Rand Eriksson as her phantom lover come to life. Or maybe the mistake had been in assuming she could handle such an overwhelming type of man if he did appear. Quite obviously she was out of her depth, and the realization was truly depressing.

As she put her key into the ignition she glanced up through the windshield, to see him standing by the door she'd just come through. His hands were deep in the pockets of his trousers. The wind tore at his hair, and his bearded chin was lifted at an aggressive angle. He might have been at the helm of a ship facing a storm at sea.

Once again Molly was reminded of Eric the Red, but this time, instead of a dashing hero filled with a soaring spirit of adventure, she saw him as the hard-drinking, roistering jarl—or earl—probing for the weakness of an empire, or of a woman, before conquering both. She felt a shiver of apprehension descend her spine, but she was determined not to let

Rand see that he had any effect on her at all. She waved casually, backed out of the parking space, and drove away at a sedate pace.

"Well, I'll be damned," Rand said, shaking his head in disbelief. He had been honest when he told her he thought she was playing hard to get. "She really wasn't fooling," he muttered as he watched her leave, his feelings mixed.

He was certain of one thing—Molly Beddingfield had written him off as uncivil and insolent. He could hardly blame her. She was a lady to her fingertips. Twelve years of bachelor life in the Navy had definitely roughened many of his smooth edges. He winced at the memory of some of the things he'd said.

His hand went to the beard, outlining the chin beneath. The way he looked had probably scared her to death too. A grin of pure mischief spread his mouth. He wondered if he could change her opinion.

Then he frowned, asking himself why it seemed so important to do that. He hunched his shoulders against the biting wind and returned to the motel, but not to the reception. As he shoved one arm into the sleeve of his coat he answered his own question. Molly Beddingfield camouflaged her sensuality well under her decorous manner, but that mouth, the slightly smoky tint in her eyes, hinted of fires banked, of desires suppressed. How he'd love to see those fires burn, those desires break free of their restraints. She'd be magnificent!

She might be a challenge, but she was also dangerous, he reminded himself sternly. By the simple fact of her existence she represented a kind of commitment. He knew he was a tender and thoughtful lover, but the other women he'd known hadn't asked for promises. No complications, no entanglements had ever marred his relationships, and he would be asking for trouble if he walked into a relationship with this woman.

That was assuming she would be willing. His grin reappeared. He'd just have to see, wouldn't he?

When Molly reached the parking lot of the museum, she turned off the ignition, then gripped the steering wheel with both hands. She looked out over the ocean for a long minute, wondering, not why she felt she'd had a narrow escape, but whether Rand Eriksson would leave her in peace.

Two

Molly's hands were not quite steady as she hung up her jacket and smoothed her hair. When she finally slid into the chair behind her desk, she heaved a sigh of relief.

"Molly?" A sharp voice from the inner office startled her.

She rose quickly and approached her boss's door. "Yes, Admiral?"

He glanced up from a file he was studying. Admiral Robert T. Jennings, U.S.N. (Ret.) resembled the stereotype of a college professor more than of a retired Navy admiral or museum director. His thinning gray hair was standing on end, and one sleeve of his tweed jacket was covered with flakes of tobacco from his ever-present pipe. He always looked to Molly as if he needed dusting off. His grizzled brows lifted as he gave her an absent smile. "How was the ceremony?"

She slid her hands into the pockets of her blazer and managed an easy smile. "Cold."

"Fine, fine, I'm glad you had a good time. Did you pick up the brochures from the printer?"

Molly cursed her own forgetfulness and the man who had caused her to forget. The errand had been the sole reason for her having taken her car rather than walking the short distance to the memorial site. "Yes," she said. "They're in my car. I'll get them."

Admiral Jennings waved a hand. "Send Tommy down for them and then come in. We need to reschedule next month's docent training program."

The rest of the afternoon flew by. Molly had no time to dwell on the memory of flashing blue eyes and a red beard, or so she told herself. The truth was, Rand Eriksson intruded on her thoughts at the most inopportune moments.

A glass-and-mahogany case for the display of the museum's most recent acquisition was delivered. As she worked with two of the interns from Old Dominion University to arrange the antique replica of a four-masted schooner, Molly's imagination just naturally placed the naval officer at the helm. But not in his gold-buttoned uniform of today. The images her mind produced were of a brawny, bronze-skinned man with broad shoulders, black breeches, and a knife between his teeth.

"Miss Beddingfield?" One of the young women graduate students was looking at her quizzically.

"Yes?"

"I asked if you want the name plate on the bow or stern."

Good Lord, she thought. She really was mixed up!

Eric the Red had given way to a swashbuckling pirate reminiscent of movie heroes from the late show. Get a hold of yourself, Molly Beddingfield, she told herself. Having a romantic and imaginative nature was one thing, but she'd better keep her daydreams in perspective.

"The stern," she said firmly.

When Molly finally finished for the day it was only five forty-five, but she was exhausted, a restless exhaustion that she didn't understand at all. She was never tired, she reminded herself as she slipped her arms into her jacket and pulled on the knitted cap.

Her life was anything but taxing. She had a job she enjoyed, a comfortable home with an adoring aunt, a placid sort of existence, in fact. Early bedtimes, plenty of exercise, an adequate social schedule including dates with men she knew well, but no emotional ties except with her family. She was happy and content. Wasn't she? Sometimes she felt restless, longing for a change, but her longings were nebulous and vague. When she tried to pin them down to specifics, they faded away.

Maybe she was coming down with the flu, she thought. She switched off the lights in the office and felt her forehead. Cool and dry. With an impatient shrug she dug in her purse for her keys and headed for the stairs.

As usual, Molly was the last to leave. The small museum, which was housed in the SeaTack Lifesaving Station building of 1925, creaked and groaned eerily as she made her way through the darkened hallway to the door leading outside. The unrelenting wind grabbed the door from her hand and crashed it against the shingled side of the building, but she finally managed to secure and lock it.

The rain had begun during the afternoon, and the crushed oyster shells that the city considered adequate paving for a parking lot were slippery and uneven, and she almost stumbled. By the time she reached her car she was breathless and drenched. Her cap and jacket smelled the way wet wool always smells—disgusting. Since she was unprotected from the hips down, her skirt was plastered to her legs. A hot bath would feel so good, she thought, and wiggled her toes inside her pumps in anticipation.

Spring storms off the Atlantic were not uncommon, but this one was fulfilling its promise to be a dilly. Molly hoped it would blow itself out that night, leaving Virginia to the tenderer mercies of warm sunshine the next day.

Aunt Jo was waiting at the door of her small corner shop on Atlantic Avenue. Holding a piece of newspaper over her head, she dashed through the rain to the curb before Molly could get out with an umbrella.

Josephine Beddingfield moved with the agility of a woman in her twenties, rather than the seventy-seven-year-old she was. Barely five feet tall in her stocking feet, she reminded Molly of a small whirlwind. Her blue eyes were shining in her wrinkled face as she dashed into the car.

"Whew!" Aunt Jo laughed, and tossed the soggy paper to the floor in the backseat. "What a storm!" She brushed ineffectually at the drops of water on her black raincoat, then pushed back the rather frazzled silver curls that tended to tumble over her forehead even in the best weather.

"You're closing early?" Molly asked, smiling affectionately. The store that was her aunt's pride was a one-woman operation. Only rarely did Aunt Jo resort to part-time help. She had two hand-lettered signs that she would hang from a nail inside the glass panel when she locked the door. Her favorite proclaimed, "Look for me when you see me," and the other read, "Playing hooky."

Her customers were indulgent about her erratic hours because of the quality of her inventory. The shop was filled to the rafters with everything needed for needlework and sewing, from fabric to zippers, from embroidery hoops to cross-stitch patterns. Her special items were beautiful knitting yarns of mohair, cashmere, and wool, and an astounding collection of buttons for every conceivable use.

"Business was nonexistent today," Aunt Jo said. "Milton's coming for dinner and I've invited a guest. We'd better stop at the market on the way home."

Milton York was the widower of Aunt Jo's best friend, and Molly was very much afraid she knew who the guest was. Would fate be so unkind? Sure, it would. She tried to keep her voice light as she pulled away from the curb. "Oh? Who is it?"

"The son of an old friend. You remember Mr. Eriksson, don't you, dear?" Aunt Jo went on blithely, unaware of Molly's quiet groan. "His son, a naval officer, has been transferred here. He came by today to say hello."

She'd just bet he had, Molly thought angrily. She wondered if he had told her aunt about their meeting. "He was at the ceremony this afternoon," she said, proud that her voice sounded neutral.

Her aunt let out an audible breath. The old fraud, Molly thought. She'd known all along.

"Yes, he told me," Aunt Jo said. "He seemed to think he might have left a bad impression on you."

"Of course he didn't. We barely talked."

Jo shot her niece a sideways glance. "He's a handsome devil, isn't he?"

"Devil" being the operative word, Molly added silently. "Is he? I'm afraid I didn't notice."

"Liar," her aunt accused fondly. "No woman could be indifferent to that one!"

She could be indifferent, Molly told herself resolutely. The reminder became a chant as she pushed the cart up and down the aisles of the supermarket, trying to ignore her aunt's chatter in praise of Rand Eriksson. All that admiration was giving her a headache. Besides, he was a sailor. Sailors were notorious for loving and leaving.

Loving? Molly shook her head. The lecture she'd given herself earlier evidently hadn't been strong enough.

When the groceries had been loaded into the backseat by a grumbling teenager in a yellow slicker, Aunt Jo suddenly became quiet. Silence was such an unnatural state with Aunt Jo, who chattered even when there was no one around to hear her, that Molly looked at her questioningly.

Aunt Jo met her eyes. "I was just wondering. . . . Do you know how very much you mean to me?" the older woman asked softly.

Being the sole sentimentalist in a family that was

only casually affectionate, Molly was stunned by the question. She knew her aunt loved her, loved all of them, but they never discussed it, never put it into words. A horrible thought struck her. "Aunt Jo! You're not . . . sick, or anything, are you?"

Instead of a flat denial, or even a laugh, Aunt Jo smiled sadly. "My dear, I'm as healthy as any seventy-seven-year-old virgin could be. It just occurred to me that I might never have told you how much I love you, and how wonderful you have been to live with me. Most young girls your age would have been chomping at the bit for a place and a life of their own, but you've sacrificed all that to take care of a dried-up old prune."

Molly chuckled, swallowing against a burning in her throat. "Old prune, indeed. What brought this on?"

Aunt Jo answered with an evasive movement of her shoulders. "Just thinking."

Molly's parents, who had been killed in an automobile accident, had left four daughters, ranging in age from six to sixteen. As the youngest, Molly had only the vaguest memories of her parents. Aunt Jo had taken all four girls into her home immediately, ignoring the suggestions of relatives that they be split up. Somehow she had known that the girls needed one another as much as they needed a home.

Molly leaned across the seat to give her aunt an impulsive hug. "I've never doubted your love, Aunt Jo. How could any of us have doubted it when you made us your family? We took over your home, disrupted your life." Her voice was husky.

"Disrupted? Oh, no, my dear. The four of you

finally gave my life some meaning. If I were never to have children of my own, my brother's children were the next best thing." She sighed. "You've been the one to give up the most."

Molly slid the key into the ignition. The rain had slackened a bit, and she hoped it would stay that way until they got home. She carefully backed into the street, searching for something to say that would dispel the mood that had put such a sad look on her aunt's face.

"But you made the ultimate sacrifice, Auntie, dear," she said teasingly. "You joined the PTA."

Aunt Jo made a face. "Even with that, I have finally come to realize that you are just an unpaid companion for an old woman."

"Nonsense! Besides, who takes care of whom? You do all the cooking, and where else could I live rent-free? With my salary, I'm grateful."

As Molly had hoped, her aunt was diverted by one of her pet peeves. "I think it is unforgivable that your salary is so meager. The custodians of our heritage should be better paid." She chattered on for the better part of five minutes, causing Molly to smile.

"Speaking of that." Aunt Jo changed the subject abruptly, looking Molly over with a keen eye. "We really must get you a new coat, dear. The red is . . . Well, with your hair . . ."

"What?" Molly asked blankly. The coat was a cast-off from one of her sisters—she didn't remember which one—who had decided it didn't suit her. It was practically new.

"Some shades of red are quite becoming to redheads," Aunt Jo said, "but that has too much orange in it."

"Aunt Jo, you know we don't have the money. I'm perfectly happy with this coat, and I won't need one for much longer this year," Molly said with a tone of finality.

The needlework shop didn't bring in much more each month than her own salary. She and Aunt Jo managed to live comfortably, but there wasn't extra money for luxuries. And a new coat, when she already had a perfectly good one, was a luxury.

"Red was fine on Louise, but it's just not your color," Aunt Jo persisted stubbornly. "I don't have to go to Richmond. We could use the money I would have spent on my trip for other things."

Molly's jaw dropped. Each year her aunt and two of her closest friends attended the Spring Needlework Show in the state capital. The event was the one thing Aunt Jo looked forward to and saved for from year to year, and her only indulgence. She was leaving in two weeks.

"You are not going to buy me a coat with your money," Molly said flatly. "For heaven's sake, Aunt Jo, it's almost April!" She pulled the car into the garage behind the house and turned off the motor with a sigh of relief. "I don't want to hear any more about it."

"Neither are your other things."

"You've lost me," Molly said as she opened the car door and climbed out. She tilted the seat forward and reached for the groceries. "If you'll carry my purse I can get both sacks."

Aunt Jo scurried ahead of her and quickly

unlocked the back door of the house. "Your clothes, Molly!" she said exasperatedly. "I'm talking about your clothes. They aren't chic enough."

Molly laughed. "Don't ever let the others hear you say that. They think their clothes are the last thing in sophistication." She turned her aunt gently in the direction of the front hall. "Go upstairs and get out of your wet things. I'll put the groceries away. Then, if you don't need any help, I'm going to soak in a hot bath."

What on earth had brought on the concern about her clothes? Molly wondered as she delved into a sodden bag and came up with an armful of cans. She had a sneaking suspicion that she knew. Rand Eriksson. Then she dismissed that idea. Surely Aunt Jo wasn't playing matchmaker. The last time had been a disaster, and she had promised never to do it again.

Molly had never been as clothes-crazy as her sisters, and, while occasionally she resented wearing their hand-me-downs, around tax time she was downright grateful. She lined up the cans on the shelves in the pantry and returned to the kitchen for more.

Later, as Molly stood in front of her closet surveying her clothes glumly, she decided her aunt was right. Her sisters were all tall, elegant creatures. Madeline, the oldest, was a silvery blonde, and the most beautiful. Beautiful enough to be on husband number three, or was it four? Molly always had to stop to think what Madeline's last name was.

Louise, the second sister, was a honey blonde. Three children hadn't ruined her figure. She kept bone-thin with constant diets and exercise routines rigorous enough for a platoon of marines.

Michelle, two years older than Molly, had golden hair. She said that her modeling career prospered because she had a flat chest, but actually the camera seemed fascinated by the alluring melancholy in her dark eyes.

The colors and styles in her sisters' wardrobes looked gorgeous with their height and coloring, but left a lot to be desired on a petite redhead. Auburn, she corrected herself automatically.

Molly gave her closet a hostile glare. Why had Aunt Jo even brought this up? She'd been content, to a degree, with her clothes, and she certainly had enough of them. Reaching in, she pulled off its hanger the first dress she touched. It was a soft wool wrap in off white that she'd inherited from Louise. Or was it Madeline? What difference did it make what she wore? She wasn't trying to impress Rand Eriksson.

Still, when she looked in her mirror a few minutes later, Molly wondered. The dress had definitely been designed for a woman who lacked her rather elaborate endowments. She pulled the fabric together over the shadow of her décolletage and fastened it with her great-grandmother's cameo. Her shining hair received a final swipe with the brush and she was ready.

The doorbell rang as she approached the head of the stairs. She hurried lightly down them, fumbled with the old-fashioned lock, and swung open the door. Then she stood stock-still with her hand on the knob, staring in blank amazement at the man before her. His appearance had once again managed to stun her into silence.

Rand was leaning casually on one forearm against the door frame. His other hand was curled into a fist on his lean hip. He was dressed in civilian clothes, a beautifully tailored camel's-hair sport coat and dark brown trousers. The jacket was open, and his stance emphasized the broad expanse of an ecru-colored shirt. His gold-and-brown-striped tie was knotted neatly at the throat but hung free, unencumbered by a tie bar or tack. However, it was not his attire that astounded her.

His beard, that lovely, thick, glorious beard, was gone! She stared at him for a long minute, speechless.

He grinned, patiently waiting for her surprise to wear off. "It's me," he finally said helpfully, and straightened.

Molly gulped and backed away a step, inviting him to enter with a sweep of her hand. "Excuse me. C-come in." She couldn't hide the dismay in her voice. That wonderful beard! At least he'd kept the moustache, but she still shook her head bemusedly as he walked past her.

Rand took her hand gently from the knob and closed the door behind him. When she still didn't move he leaned down until his face was inches from hers. "What's the matter?" he asked.

"Your beard," she answered weakly.

He put both hands on her shoulders and searched her expression. "You really liked it!" he said incredulously.

"Yes. It was . . ." She had to grope for a word, and

blurted it out before examining it carefully. "Romantic." She hastily added an irrational explanation. "You looked like what you are."

"Ah-h-h," he said, understanding at last. His eyes mellowed to a soft, summery blue. "Correction. I looked like what *you* think I am."

When she didn't answer, he touched her cheek with his fingertips. The small caress sent a warm shiver down her neck, and suddenly she was numbed by the same spell he'd cast that afternoon. "A young jarl?" he asked, using the very term she'd thought of earlier. "Is that the way you see me?"

She swallowed and nodded.

His shoulders moved slightly under his coat. "If that's what you want." His arm slid around her waist, pulling her slowly against his hard length. The hand at her face raked into her hair to hold her head steady while his descended.

His deliberately slow movements certainly gave her plenty of warning, she thought fleetingly, and wondered why she had no intention of heeding that warning.

She felt his warm breath, sweet on her lips, for an instant before his kiss blotted out everything else. The sensation was unlike anything Molly had ever experienced. His mouth was mobile and magnetic, drawing any resistance from her slight body before inhibition could provoke a withdrawal.

Her hand touched his chest tentatively, but in compliance, not opposition. Her subconscious had only been waiting, she realized in an illuminating flash. She had wanted this from the first moment she'd seen him. Her lips parted to admit the soft exploration of his tongue, and when she felt it nudge her own, she responded eagerly.

Her reaction kindled a sudden, unmistakable flame of arousal in Rand. His arm tightened about her, bringing her into relentless contact with every inch of his body from thigh to chest. His mouth was bold now, and the heartbeat against her breast surged into a stronger rhythm.

Her hands burrowed under his jacket and around to his back to explore the muscles there. They were iron-hard beneath her fingers. He smelled of soap and an after-shave reminiscent of sailors and the sea. She was lost to sensation and time. When her neck would no longer support her head, she succumbed gratefully to the support of his hand.

Finally, after an eternity, he lifted his head. He released his hold on her and cradled her face in his warm hands.

Acting on instinct alone, she urged her heavy eyelids up, wanting to see his face, wanting to see if he was as affected by the kiss as she was. His eyes were blurred in bewilderment as he stared at her, the chaos of her own reeling senses reflected clearly in his gaze. His breathing was quick and loud in the quiet of the dimly-lit hall. At least it wasn't only herself, she thought dazedly.

His next words affirmed her thoughts. "I knew it," he breathed, as his thumbs scraped tenderly across her cheeks. "I knew you'd taste like heaven, your body would feel so good against me. And you knew it, too, didn't you, sweet Molly?"

She gave him a misty smile, and he groaned softly

and wrapped her in his arms again. "I'm glad I shaved," he whispered into her hair.

"Why?" she murmured.

"Because I plan to do a lot of this and I wouldn't want to scratch your lovely skin." He urged her head back until it rested in the hollow of his shoulder. "Anywhere," he added with unmistakable meaning.

Molly was surprised at her own acceptance of the knowing suggestion in that statement. It didn't matter that she'd never reacted this quickly and completely to a man before. It didn't matter that this afternoon she'd tried to tell herself that Rand was danger walking around in a fantastic body. It didn't even matter that he was a Navy officer and probably had a girl in every port. The only thing that mattered to her at this moment was that his arms were strong around her, that he felt the same way she did. The feeling was so . . . so right, and she had no intention of questioning it.

Just then they both heard footsteps on the front porch, approaching the door behind them. Milton, Molly thought sadly. She would have liked to have one more kiss. She leaned back in Rand's arms to see her desire mirrored in his blue eyes.

"Tomorrow," he said huskily, quickly, before they could be interrupted. "Will you spend tomorrow with me?"

"Yes. Of course I will."

A roguish dimple, which had been hidden in the beard, showed itself when he smiled his satisfaction. She couldn't resist touching it.

Rand caught her hand and turned his face into her

palm, leaving a tender kiss there as a talisman of what was to come, of tomorrow.

The ringing of the doorbell drew them apart. With the loss of Rand's warmth, Molly felt as if she had lost a part of herself.

Three

"Come in, Milton," Molly said, swinging the door wide to admit the distinguished-looking man. Her spirits were soaring somewhere up around the ceiling, and her voice reflected the jubilant effervescence percolating through her bloodstream. Rand wanted to see her tomorrow, she thought. He wanted to spend the day with her.

Milton kissed her cheek, eyeing her strangely. "Good evening, Molly."

The older man was slightly hard of hearing, and Molly automatically raised her voice. "I'd like you to meet Rand Eriksson. Rand, this is our neighbor and very good friend, Milton York."

The men shook hands while Molly simply watched, smiling benignly on them both but thinking only of the moments before the doorbell rang.

"May I take your coat, sir?" Rand asked after a moment's pause.

His offer brought Molly's thoughts back sharply from the memory of the kiss. Good Lord, how long would she have stood there grinning like a mesmerized idiot while poor Milton dripped on the worn Persian carpet? "I'll take it," she blurted too loudly, earning herself another strange look, from both men this time. But Rand's eyes were twinkling with amused satisfaction, while Milton simply looked confused.

You think you're confused, she thought as she hung Milton's wet coat on the hall tree. Her smile wavered. "Why don't you both go into the parlor while I see if I can help Aunt Jo? Make yourselves at home," she mumbled, and escaped to the kitchen.

"Did I hear the doorbell?" Jo asked when Molly entered the kitchen. Her aunt's gray curls had been brushed into a neat halo and Jo was wearing her favorite dress, Molly noted absently, a soft wool challis patterned in several shades of blue. A bib apron of lemon yellow protected the garment from spatters.

"Yes," she answered abruptly as she collapsed into a kitchen chair. "They're both here."

"Good. I'm just about done. Did you offer them a drink?"

Molly knew that the question was rhetorical. She had been reared on the amenities, and courtesy was second nature to her. Or had been until tonight. Tonight she might have been the world's most inexperienced hostess. And all because of one kiss. She looked at her aunt, busy at the stove, and there must have been an expression of something akin to horror on her face.

When Jo turned from the stove to see why she hadn't answered, her own jaw went slack. The spoon she was holding dropped, bouncing once and splattering liquid over the floor. "Molly dear, what's the matter?"

"He did it to me again," Molly almost wailed.

Carefully avoiding the puddle at her feet, Jo approached Molly. "Who did what? Molly, you're flushed. Aren't you feeling well?"

Molly's hands twisted into impotent fists at her sides. "That damned sailor!" she erupted.

Jo recoiled as though she'd been shot. "Molly! Such language! Wha-what did he do?" she whispered.

Molly could easily understand her aunt's reaction. She'd never cursed in front of her aunt before in her life, but contrarily she was experiencing a rare feeling of exhilaration at having stepped out of her role of southern lady so completely. "He kissed me," she explained.

Jo seemed to recall herself and closed her mouth. She picked the spoon up off the floor and went to the sink to wash it, avoiding Molly's eyes all the time. "Well, you've certainly been kissed before," she said mildly. "So what's the problem?"

"Not like that. I guarantee you, not like that." Molly bounced up from the chair, grabbed a sponge from the counter, and wiped up the spill with more vigor than was necessary. "And he made me say I'd spend the day with him tomorrow," she added, tossing the sponge into the sink.

"He *made* you?"

Molly sank back into the chair, all the sudden defiance draining out of her in a rush, leaving her oddly unsure. "Aunt Jo, believe me, it was against my better judgment." Molly shook her head. "Or it is now that my judgment's returned. At the time . . . He's a very compelling man, and audacious," she finished in a whisper, her eyes wide as she stared at her aunt. "I'm not sure what I should do."

Jo looked at her for a long minute, then turned away, dipping the clean spoon into the pot. "Well, just tell him you've changed your mind," she suggested.

Molly's chin came up with a jerk. "No," she answered immediately. "I want to go," she added, but her tone was vague and troubled. "Isn't that about the stupidest thing you've ever heard? I really want to go!"

"Then go, and have fun. It's about time someone came along who could shake you up a bit. You certainly need that," Jo said with asperity. "I liked Rand from the minute I met him. I don't want you to misunderstand, but lately I've noticed that you're becoming more and more complacent about your life, Molly. And you can be pretty intimidating when you want to."

It was Molly's turn to be shocked. "Aunt Jo!"

"Don't pretend to be insulted." Jo grinned devilishly. "I know it's a protective facade. I've even used it myself on occasion. But not many men can stand up to you, Molly. I've watched you twist them around your finger like so much yarn, but you never seem to be really involved. It's as though you're standing off to the side in all your relationships, and the men you choose to date are always those whom you can lead around by the nose or dispose of with a word. I don't think you're going to get rid of this one so easily."

Had she really been that intimidating? Molly wondered. Or had she known that when the right person came along she wouldn't be able to get away with it? Even after her stringent put-down this afternoon, Rand had persisted. Did that mean that he was the right person? How crazy! She barely knew the man. "The men I date are gentlemen," she defended weakly.

"So is Rand. But the accent's on the 'man' rather than the 'gentle.'"

"You can say that again," muttered Molly wryly.

"Even your very proper sisters knew when to step down off their pedestals, Molly," Jo said gently.

Molly's eyes were fixed on her aunt, but she didn't see the diminutive woman. Her main concern was whether she could handle her own reactions. She often felt like the nineteenth-century freak Rand thought her to be. It was a hateful feeling to be so out of step with her contemporaries, to be so old-fashioned and formal. But she was a product of a life that circumstances had forced on her, and those circumstances hadn't changed.

The wind rattled the door, bringing both of them back to the present. "The storm's building," Aunt Jo said. "You'd better get back into the parlor and offer our guests a drink, Molly. I'll join you in a moment."

"Okay," Molly murmured in a desultory voice, and rose. At the door to the hall she turned back. "Do you really think I need shaking up?" she asked quietly.

"Or waking up," her aunt corrected with a gentle smile. "Furthermore, I think this 'damn Yankee' has come along at just the right time. Relax and enjoy it, my dear."

Molly tried to come up with a rebuttal, but her aunt went on before she could think of anything. "Our guests, Molly," she reminded.

If only she could relax and enjoy having Rand there, Molly thought. If only she could let herself go. Her aunt didn't know that it wasn't just her natural reserve that made her keep men at arm's length. Once she had let those barriers down halfway, once she had thought in terms of love, for a brief while. But the man had made it very clear that Molly's responsibility for her aunt was not one that he cared to share. That had hurt, but she had an idea that if Rand had been that man, the pain would have been even worse, maybe impossible to bear.

Milton, who knew his way around the house as well as its occupants, had done the honors of pouring drinks, and the two men were talking like old friends. They both rose as Molly entered the room.

Rand eyed her with affection. "Can I fix something for you, Miss Beddingfield?"

She shot him a suspicious glance, but there was no sarcasm in his smile. "No, thank you." She didn't need an alcoholic beverage for stimulation. On the other hand, a sherry might calm her nerves. "I'll have a sherry," she said, and sank gratefully into a chair.

If Rand noticed that she was rattled to the point of inconsistency, he was wise enough not to comment.

"Thank you," she said, as she accepted the small crystal glass from him. She avoided his eyes as adroitly as she avoided touching his fingers, and focused her attention on the older man. "Did you happen to hear a weather report this evening, Milton?"

"Yes. Blackberry winter, you know. Next week we'll probably need air-conditioning, but tonight I'm afraid we're in for quite a storm."

As though reinforcing his opinion, the lights flickered briefly, but didn't go out. Three pairs of eyes automatically studied the chandelier.

"Did I see the lights blink?"

Both men rose as Jo entered the room.

"You saw them," Milton said. "I hope the electricity doesn't go off, not until after dinner, anyway. Bourbon and branch, Jo?"

"Please, Milton. Rand, how are you this evening?" She sat at one end of the Victorian love seat and accepted with a warm smile the glass that the older man presented to her.

"Fully recovered, thank you, Miss Beddingfield."

Molly looked blank. "Recovered?"

"Please call me Jo. Miss Beddingfield is such a mouthful."

Still standing, Rand nodded in response to the suggestion before he answered Molly. "There was an authentic arctic chill in the atmosphere at the ceremony this afternoon, wouldn't you agree?" he said.

She glared up at him, apprised very efficiently by the gleam in his eyes that he wasn't referring to the weather. "Was there? I didn't notice."

"Oh, yes." His gaze dropped deliberately to her lips, and she could feel her mouth and throat drying in reaction. "Sometimes you have to take drastic measures to warm yourself after such exposure." His voice was low and deep and brimming with suggestion.

Jo choked slightly on her drink and dabbed at her lips with a tiny linen napkin. "Is this the first time you've seen the ceremony, Rand?"

He moved to stand with one elbow resting on the mantel, allowing Molly to breathe again. "No, I came once before, years ago, when I was at the University in Charlottesville, but I'm afraid I don't remember much of the story." His grin activated the dimple in his cheek. "Except the part where your grandmother saved my grandfather's life."

"Remind me to show you the portrait. I don't know how she did it. Alice Beddingfield was a tiny little thing compared to the rest of the women in our family, like Molly."

"And yourself," Molly added, turning to Aunt Jo. Her eyes implored her aunt to desist. She was never comfortable being the center of attention, and with Rand Eriksson in the room, "uncomfortable" became "nerve-wracking."

"And myself," agreed Jo with an innocent smile. "But I'm not a redhead. That's why Molly inherited the brooch."

"The brooch?" Rand asked.

"The one Molly's wearing."

Molly almost groaned aloud as her aunt's statement brought Rand's gaze directly to her breasts and the cameo that held her dress together. His gaze lingered for a long time. If anything was more erotic than Rand staring at her mouth, it was Rand staring at her breasts. Aunt Jo was throwing her to the wolves, she thought fiercely, and she was tempted to wring her aunt's neck.

"I'll let her tell you about it while I put the finishing

touches on our dinner," Jo said. She drained the last of the liquid in her glass and stood. "No, I don't need any help," she said when all three of them moved, two out of politeness, one in panic. "Dinner will be ready in about five minutes, if anyone would like another drink." She sailed out of the room.

Bless Milton's heart, and his hearing aid, Molly thought as he took up the story where Jo had left off. "Alice stipulated in her will that the brooch should go to the next redheaded female in the family, and there wasn't one until Molly was born."

Rand sauntered over to her chair and actually leaned over. "Interesting design," he murmured, his lips twitching.

"You wretch!" she whispered fiercely.

"Guilty as charged," he whispered back.

She reluctantly returned his grin. Just then the lights flickered again, and Rand straightened, breaking the link of awareness between them. Molly laughed nervously and took a small sip of her sherry. She had just set her glass down on the table beside her when everything went black. "Oh, no!"

She heard a sound of dismay from Milton and a tolerant laugh from Rand.

"Don't worry. We have plenty of candles," she told them as she got to her feet, holding on to the padded arm of the chair.

"Where are they?" asked Rand from out of the darkness. "I'll get them."

"You'd never find them." She gave her eyes a moment to adjust to the dark, but it was so black that, even when her pupils were dilated, she couldn't make out the shape of the hand in front of her face.

She had to feel her way to the cabinet where the candles were kept. Pulling out the top drawer, she rummaged among the various items until her fingers touched smooth wax. "I have it. Now, if I can just find the matches . . ."

"Let me help." Rand's voice was close to her ear, and his hands rested lightly at her waist.

She almost jumped out of her skin. How had he gotten so close without her hearing him? He had to have cat's eyes to be able to see so well in the dark. She felt the now-familiar weakness in her knees as the heat from his large body encircled her. "I don't need any help," she protested in a whisper as she tried to wiggle free from his loose grip.

Instead of obeying her silent demand he swept her hair aside with one hand. His other arm circled her waist like a bar of heat beneath her breasts, bringing her hard against him. His lips found a vulnerable spot at her nape, where he left a quick, burning kiss before releasing her. She caught her breath with an audible gasp. "Don't," she hissed.

"Rand? Molly? Is there anything wrong?" Milton asked.

"No, nothing," she hastily assured him.

Rand reached around her to find the packet of matches in the drawer. "Here we are."

Molly leaned heavily against the cabinet for a moment, wishing Rand would move away so she could breathe without the scent of his cologne overwhelming her senses. Instead he struck the match, cupping it in his big hand to preserve the fragile flame. The room took shape again. She turned to find herself only inches away from him.

His eyes, glowing sea-blue, bright with an unmistakable message, met hers over the tiny blaze. "The candle," he reminded her softly, his breath warm and sweet on her upturned face.

She felt the heat rise from her chin and wondered if the singeing sensation in her cheeks was from the match or if she was actually blushing.

"If you don't hurry up, Red, I'm going to burn my fingers," he said.

"Oh! Yes, I . . . You . . ." She clamped her jaws together before she could make a bigger fool of herself. The candle was still clenched tightly in her fist. Wondering why it hadn't melted to soup in her hand, she touched the wick to the tip of the match. "There," she said with great relief, and turned back to the drawer as Rand shook the match to extinguish the flame.

She pulled out candlesticks of all sorts, fit the taper she was holding into a double-branched brass candelabrum, and lined the rest of the candles up on the cabinet. "I'd better take one of these back to Aunt Jo," she said.

"I'll take it to her," said Milton, appearing out of the shadows behind Rand.

Molly hesitated. It would be foolish to argue, no matter how much she wanted breathing room. "Thank you, Milton," she said finally, fitting another candle into a glass holder. She lit it from the one already burning, and offered it to him. She was dismayed to see that her hand was trembling so obviously.

Milton seemed not to notice. He disappeared

through the door to the hall, calling, "I'm coming, Jo."

Rand chuckled under his breath. "You didn't want to be left alone with me. Do I get to you, Miss Beddingfield?"

"I don't know what you're talking about." Wonderful, Molly. When you don't know what to say, revert to the trite.

He took her by the shoulders, turning her to face him. His touch was gentle but firm. If he'd mocked her, she would have punched him in the jaw in an unladylike manner, which would have truly shocked him, but he didn't. His voice was deep and tender, and she felt herself responding to his smile. "Let's go back to where we were when the doorbell rang." He tucked a strand of her hair behind her ear, and his fingers lingered there for a moment. "If I have to, I can repeat the lesson."

"You'd better not," she whispered. "If Milton walked in, that kind of demonstration would throw the poor man into total confusion."

"Not your aunt?"

Remembering the lecture in the kitchen, Molly shook her head ruefully. She dipped her chin, turning her face to one side to look up at Rand through thick lashes. Her smile tilted slightly. "I'm afraid Aunt Jo would be delighted," she said softly.

Suddenly she was pulled hard against him. His arms wrapped her close and his laugh rumbled up from his chest. "You're flirting with me!" he said, rocking her lightly in his arms. "The very proper Miss Beddingfield is flirting!"

Slightly dazed by the sensation of being plastered

against his powerful body once more, Molly hid her face under his chin. "Am I?" she asked huskily.

But Rand wouldn't allow her to hide. He cradled her face in his hands, his fingers tangling in her hair, and forced her to meet his eyes.

Her own hands came up to grasp his wrists, meaning to pull them away, but instead she was once again caught in his blue gaze, its effect made more mesmerizing by the glow of candlelight.

His eyes bore deeply into hers, pressing for something, urging her forward toward an unexplored, exotic place. She felt as if a chrysalis were cracking, breaking up around her, letting in fresh warmth and new needs, strange and frightening needs.

Her expression must have told him of the transformation going on inside her, and her fear of it. "You certainly are flirting," he murmured encouragingly, "and I love it."

She shook her head slightly. "I'm not good at—"

His gentle kiss rested on her lips for a brief, wonderful moment, halting the rest of her words. "Oh, yes." His voice was thick and husky. "You're very good. Please don't stop."

The last sentence was uttered with such sincerity that she had to swallow before she could answer. "I—you . . . Perhaps you'd better let me go."

"Okay," he said agreeably enough, but he seemed to be caught in an emotional maze too.

Her hands tugged on his wrists, and he blinked once, dropped them immediately, and stepped back from her. "Sorry," he said with a smile.

She deliberately instilled brightness into her voice.

"Now I have to spread a little light. Would you help me put more candles around?"

His slow grin revealed his beautiful white teeth below the full moustache. Before he could answer, though, there was a tremendous crash from the front porch. "What the hell . . . ?" Rand swung around and was halfway across the room before Molly could even react. He reached the outside door at the same time that she stepped into the hall. As the rain hit him full force she was right behind him, knowing far better than he what had caused the crash.

The wicker porch furniture was being tumbled about by the tremendous force of the wind. Several pieces had already landed on the grass, beyond the porch rail.

"Get back inside before you get blown away too," he ordered.

"Don't be silly," she shouted over a howling gust. "It's my fault. I should have remembered to put everything away."

Suddenly she was hit in the face by something heavy and clinging. She screamed, fighting the folds of whatever seemed intent on smothering her. At last she managed to pull it away, but not before she was gasping for breath. It was a garment of some kind.

"You found my raincoat," Rand said. "Good. Where do you want this stuff?" He had a chair in one hand and a plant stand in the other, and was positively soaked.

She tossed the sodden garment through the door behind her, "There's an offset around the corner that's protected from the wind," she directed, and hurried down the steps to grab a settee, trying to keep it from blowing into the street. Her long hair swirled across her face, and she impatiently pushed it out of her eyes with a forearm.

Rand was back in seconds. "Dammit! I told you to get inside. Look at you. You're drenched."

"Don't be ridiculous. I've done this many times. Besides, you're drenched too."

With a muttered curse he manhandled the settee away from her and lifted it over his head, carrying it effortlessly up the steps and around the house.

Molly picked up a baby chair and another plant stand. She met him at the bottom of the steps with her haul, and he took it from her. "Molly, dammit . . .!" But she had already turned away to salvage the only other remaining piece, a huge platform rocker belonging to her grandfather that she wouldn't have thought a typhoon could move. She was struggling with it when Rand returned.

"You are the most stubborn female I've ever met," he yelled as he grabbed the other arm of the rocker. "What the hell do you use for brains?"

She was soaked to the skin and cold, and this overbearing idiot had the nerve to question her sense of responsibility? She dropped her side of the chair and faced him with her fists planted on her hips, chin thrust out boldly. "Guts!" she yelled back. "What do you use?"

They both froze for an endless minute, glaring at each other across the seat of her grandfather's favorite chair. Slowly, through the curtain of rain, she saw Rand's scowl evaporate, modify itself into a hesitant smile. His gaze traveled down the length of her and back up, taking in the saturated dress that clung to her every curve and the wet hair that fell over her shoulders like a soggy blanket. He shook his head and the smile grew to a grin.

Molly looked at the drooping moustache, which held tiny beads of water; the red hair, plastered to his forehead; the fine camel's-hair jacket, which seemed to be shrinking before her eyes; and laughed, a short yip of sound that she tried to catch with a hand over her mouth, but didn't succeed.

Suddenly they were both laughing, shouting with glee. "Look at you!" she shrieked, pointing a finger at him, and doubled up holding her side.

He spread his hands and shrugged. "Look at you!" was his rejoinder. "Miz Beddingfield is wetter than a mad hen!" he hooted in the worst southern accent she'd ever heard.

For some reason the fake drawl and the silly misquote sent her off into further peals of laughter. "You're crazy!"

"Crazy, am I?" Rand was around the chair like lightning, and when he reached for her she threw her arms around his neck. His arms wound tightly around her waist, lifting her off the ground, twirling her around with the exuberance of their shared mirth.

In that exultant moment Molly felt freer, younger, than she'd ever felt in her life. Letting her head fall back she stuck out her tongue to taste the rainwater. And he took the taste from her mouth, over and over, in short thirsty kisses. "You're wonderful," he whispered against her lips.

"So are you."

Their eyes met, and the electricity arced between

them. Her lips parted willingly and her arms tightened around his neck, clinging as his mouth crushed hers.

The rain, swept wildly by the unrelenting wind, pelted their faces, their bodies, but neither of them noticed. They could have been standing on the outer edge of a hurricane for all they knew. Desire, made even stronger by the unexpected turbulence of passion, was the only thing either of them was conscious of at the moment.

Rand was the first to come to his senses. Reluctantly he broke off the kiss, resting his forehead against hers. "Molly. Oh, Molly," he breathed. Still holding her several inches off the ground with one strong arm, he smoothed her hair away from her face with his other hand. "I'd better get you inside before you catch pneumonia," he said shakily. He swung her up into his arms.

Her head found a natural resting place between his jaw and shoulder, and she looped her arms around his neck. "The chair . . ." she said vaguely.

"I'll come back for it," he growled, and his lips brushed her temple.

Thirty minutes later the small dinner party regrouped in front of a warm, glowing fire in the grate. Jo had pronounced the dining room too chilly and spread a mahogany card table in the parlor with a white cloth.

Now she fussed over the table, straightening a fork, aligning a napkin. Salad plates with individual slices of aspic on crisp lettuce were to the left of each place setting. A silver basket held hot poppy-seed rolls and sweet, creamy butter, and homemade green-tomato pickles were arranged on flat crystal plates.

Molly, huddled in a corner of the sofa with her feet curled under her, pinched her nose to hold back a sneeze. "Can't I help, Aunt Jo?" she offered.

"You and Rand stay close to the fire," Jo instructed. "Honestly, I've never seen two soggier humans in my life. Milton and I can manage." She blushed. "That is if you don't mind, Milton."

"Of course I don't mind, Jo," Milton said gently.

Something in his tone caught Molly's instant attention, something she had never heard before, and Aunt Jo's blush was a dead giveaway. Her aunt never blushed. A speculative gleam lit Molly's eyes as she watched them leave the room. Aunt Jo and Milton? Well, why not?

Milton had taken every opportunity to help Aunt Jo tonight, including placing the pots and pans under the leaks in the roof. Molly smiled at the memory of her aunt sweetly, if purposefully, supervising him. She started to share her thoughts with Rand before she realized suddenly that her aunt was no concern of his. That was a mistake she would never make again.

Aunt Jo was right about the dining room. The whole house was beginning to lose its heat. Molly unfolded her feet and stood. Moving with studied nonchalance, she knelt beside Rand on the floor in front of the fireplace and held out her hands to the warmth. Without seeming too obvious, she looked sideways at him, only to find her gaze caught again in the blue depths of his eyes.

She dropped her gaze quickly, but his virile image was imprinted on her brain. His hair had dried quickly, and Aunt Jo had found one of her father's ancient dressing gowns for him to wear. A remnant of a finer and more prosperous age, the maroon brocade covered Rand only enough to satisfy decency, but still lent him the impressive demeanor of a Grand Duke.

The only thing that detracted from the splendor was his feet stretched out toward the fire. Grandfather's slippers hadn't fit at all, so Aunt Jo had come up with a pair of one-size-fits-all tennis socks that belonged to Louise's husband.

Rand caught Molly looking at his feet. He wiggled his toes and grinned. "Ruins the image, doesn't it?"

She laughed nervously. "A little. But you don't look as bad as I do."

She was bundled up in a lavender fleece robe of Madeline's that did even less for her coloring than the red reefer. Without electricity she couldn't dry her hair, so she had wrapped it turban style in a towel.

"You look very . . . touchable," he said softly. "Very, very sexy."

Her eyes dropped under the determination in his. Surely he must know that she had never gone through an emotional storm like the one outside, she thought. It had left her keyed-up, excited, but had also served to reinforce her doubts. She had broken free of the chrysalis, but what did she use now for self-protection?

"Tomorrow we're going to talk, Molly." Rand went on in that same gentle tone.

She traced the line of the zipper in her robe. "About what?" she asked lightly.

"About us," he answered. "About all the things you and I have been doing in our lives up until now. And about where we go from here."

She lifted her gaze to meet his. The desire there had been banked for now. It lay beneath the surface, ready to flare at the least spark, but was subdued. His eyes held reassurance instead, a certainty of feelings, and a promise to temper the passion with friendship.

The unspoken promise earned him a thankful smile and, though he didn't know it, the beginnings of her trust. "All right," she agreed. "We'll talk tomorrow."

Milton preceded Aunt Jo into the room, carrying a large tureen. The delicious smell of ragout permeated the room. He placed his burden carefully in the center of the table, and Aunt Jo said, "Dinner is served." There was a becoming flush to her cheeks.

"Jo's ragout is something to savor, Rand," said Milton. "You're in for a treat."

"Wonderful. I'm starving." He got to his feet and put out a hand to help Molly up. Before he released her he squeezed her fingers lightly and smiled.

The meal was eaten in silence until the edge was taken off their appetites. Milton refilled their wineglasses and asked, "Where are you staying, Rand?"

"I'm at a motel on the next block," he answered. "But I have a couple of weeks' leave coming and a hankering to look out on the ocean, so starting tomorrow I'm going house-hunting. That is, if I can talk Molly into showing me the best beach-front areas."

Molly touched her napkin to her mouth. "There are some beautiful apartments north of here, on Oceanfront."

"Not an apartment. I've lived in apartments for too long. I want a real house, with a lawn to mow and shrubbery to prune."

Molly was surprised that a bachelor like Rand would want that kind of responsibility. She frowned, searching her memory. "There aren't many houses to rent on the beach."

"I plan to buy," he added, surprising her further. "I've also never owned a home. It never seemed practical, before now."

She looked at him for a hint as to the meaning of that statement, but he wasn't giving a thing away.

Jo sipped her wine and looked speculatively from one to the other of them. "Molly has a . . . friend in the real estate business. Maybe you should call Lee in the morning, Molly."

Molly's eyes shot loving daggers at her aunt. "Certainly. I'm sure Lee would know of something."

Only an idiot would have missed the amusement in Jo's voice, and Rand wasn't an idiot. "Lee. Male or female Lee?" he asked with a grin.

"Male," Molly said shortly.

"That's settled, then," said Jo. "But until you find a place, Rand, I think you should move in here. I would never be able to face your mother if I let you remain in a motel, when we have the master bedroom downstairs just sitting empty."

Molly had to bite back a gasp of shock and dismay. Shock because the master bedroom was her grandfather's shrine, and dismay because her aunt Jo was being excessively obvious, right down to the overdone flutter of southern feminine helplessness. Matchmaking was one thing, but moving him right into the house . . .!

"Aunt Jo, aren't you forgetting your trip?" she reminded her aunt sweetly, but with a hint of steel in her voice. "You leave in two weeks for Richmond. Do you think it would look right? Rand and me here alone?" She batted her eyes. Two could play at this game.

Jo frowned her annoyance at being caught playacting. "Well, he can stay until I leave," she said bluntly. "Besides, I have some shrubbery that needs pruning." She turned to Rand with an innocent smile that didn't fool anyone. "You can practice on our yard work, to see if it really is as appealing as you anticipate."

Milton was trying his best to keep from grinning, and Rand swallowed his laughter with a sip of wine.

Molly kicked him under the table, but he ignored her. "I would love to stay here, Jo," he said with a perfectly straight face, "if you're sure it wouldn't be too much of an inconvenience."

"No inconvenience at all. You can move in tomorrow. Molly will help you."

Molly opened her mouth to protest, but closed it again at a really strong glare from her aunt and a squeeze of the hand in her lap from Rand. They would talk about this tomorrow, too, she resolved.

Later, as Molly stood at her bedroom window brushing her hair, she gazed down at the flashing neon sign of the restaurant across the street, a garish reminder that their house sat right in the middle of a commercial strip. Aunt Jo's home was one of the few private residences remaining along this stretch of Atlantic Avenue. The value of the property, as well as that of her aunt's small shop, had risen astronomically, and the taxes had risen in proportion. Molly tried, she *really* tried, not to resent the fact that they were sitting on real estate worth a lot of money. Sometimes she wished . . . No! They might be living on the edge of poverty, but it was genteel poverty, and Aunt Jo had been so good to them all. How could she ask her to give up the home she'd lived in for seventy-seven years?

A smaller place, easier to keep and less expensive, would be nice, but it wouldn't be home. Molly's grandfather had built this house, and she loved it, too, even if the noise of the summer traffic was dreadful. Even if the juniper shingles looked like an anachronism among the plate-glass-and-concrete block of the motel strip, it was home.

Beyond the neon lights the sea tumbled wildly against the shore. Molly's thoughts returned to Rand. And to Erik and Alice. As she had done so many times before, Molly pictured the scene that long-ago day in March.

In the late 1800s no seawall separated or protected the signs of civilization from the elements, and only a few buildings had dotted the beach. One of them had been the opulent Princess Anne Hotel. Three stories high, it had stretched two full blocks and easily dominated the landscape. A glass-enclosed sun porch had overlooked the ocean. Was that where Alice had stood when she first spied the young seaman struggling against the fury of the storm-tossed sea? Molly wondered. It had been late in the afternoon, almost evening. Had Alice already dressed for dinner, in rustling silk over ruffled petticoats? Was she surrounded by other women in their formal gowns, men in the required tuxedos? Had the chamber quartet begun to play for the evening's dancing?

What was he like, Alice? What was the other Eriksson like? Was he bearded, dashing, handsome . . . dangerous? Did he have this magnetism that threatened your peace of mind the way Rand does mine? You were engaged to great-grandfather Beddingfield, but were you tempted by a Viking, even a little bit?

Molly sighed deeply and resumed her brushing. The rhythmic strokes as well as the constant rhythm of the waves finally soothed the turmoil inside her. She tossed the brush at a nearby chair, not even noticing when it fell to the floor, and climbed between sweet-smelling, lavender-scented sheets.

Alice, you've provided me with a dilly of a legacy. Whatever happens, it's on your head, old girl.

Four

Rand settled Molly into the bucket seat of a luxurious black sports car that would have paid the taxes on the Beddingfield house for a year. The car even smelled expensive.

She swept her chocolate-colored twill skirt inside and he closed the door. Her long hair was tied back neatly with a pink scarf that matched the cotton sweater she was wearing. For once the color was becoming; Aunt Jo had knit the sweater as her Christmas present.

Rand waved good-bye to her aunt, who was standing on the porch beaming at them, and circled the car to join her. Without saying a word he turned the key in the ignition and the engine roared to life.

Aunt Jo had once again been too obvious, bless her heart, Molly thought. She had fussed over Rand relentlessly. Had he had breakfast? . . . They were looking forward to having a man in the house again. . . . She would expect him to pack his bags and return with Molly in time for dinner.

He was probably irritated, Molly thought with no remorse. His jaw seemed very square to her, very defensive, and she had to remind herself again that if he was uncomfortable with the situation, it was his own fault. He'd asked for it when he'd agreed so willingly to come to stay with them. She was certain that he was convinced she was a woman on the prowl for a husband, and that her aunt was her cohort in the hunt.

Molly's emotions were close to the surface this morning. A scratch and their raw sensitivities would be revealed to the stinging air of reality. But the really unsettling thought was that she wasn't sure what those emotions were.

Rand excited her. He encouraged her to let go of all the restrictive refinements that had kept her safe for so many years, but at the same time he seemed ready, even eager, to support her when the props were removed. She couldn't decide whether his encouragement was only a method of seduction by a man of experience—experience that she admittedly lacked.

She slid a glance to his strong profile. He was dressed casually, in khakis and a soft blue V-neck sweater that looked like cashmere. His blue-and-white-striped shirt was open at the throat. She sighed and turned her head to stare out of the window. The storm had passed during the night, and the day sparkled with sunshine and the clean, washed look that follows a rain.

They had gone only one block when Rand turned

into the parking lot of a savings and loan bank. Molly looked at him in surprise.

"They're closed on Sunday," she said.

He pulled up the emergency brake and switched off the engine. "Of course they are," he said smoothly. He turned toward her, one long arm across the back of her seat. "I'm not here to open an account."

"Then why . . .?" Her voice trailed off under the force of his blue gaze.

"Because I am going to kiss you, and it's safer to do that when the car isn't moving." The hand behind her head dropped to her shoulder, urging her closer.

Her hand went instinctively to his broad chest, holding him off. "You're too sure of yourself."

"Ha! That's what you think." His smile was crooked, and he paid no attention to her resistance. "You're not sure enough."

"Of course I am."

"Listen, I don't know what dreams went on in your pretty head last night, what demons your imagination conceived, but I'm not going to let you withdraw into that cloister of propriety you throw up to keep everyone out. Last night, out in the storm, I thought that the proper Miss Beddingfield had matured into Molly, but this morning she seems to be back. I like Molly a hell of a lot better."

Her eyes were wide, searching. "Matured?" That was a strange choice of verb.

He pulled her closer, until their eyes were only inches apart. "Matured is a good word," he said firmly. "Miss Beddingfield seems to me to be a bit childlike, still dressed up in her white gloves and party manners. Molly is a sensual, desirable woman, brave enough to take a chance on her feelings."

The strong beating of his heart beneath her hand accelerated as his gaze fell to her lips. His eyes darkened, but he didn't kiss her. "Come back to me, Molly," he urged quietly.

She was puzzled for a minute, then her lips curved in understanding. Rand was issuing an unspoken challenge to discover whether or not she was brave enough to take the last step herself.

Yes, she certainly was. The devils and demons that had haunted her dreams last night were only imps that chided her for hesitating. Aunt Jo had been absolutely right when she'd said that with Rand Eriksson, the emphasis was on the man. He was the someone sent by destiny, by fortune, or maybe by Alice, to shake her out of her shell of complacency. She'd decided sometime during the night that that complacency was awfully boring. Her eyes raised to tangle with his.

His expression softened, as if he were reading her mind.

"Rand . . ."

"Yes, darling?" His brow lifted in amused inquiry.

Darling? she thought. "Miss Beddingfield hasn't even been in the car this morning."

He took a long breath and smiled tenderly at her. "It may take me a while to be able to tell the difference," he said, tucking a strand of hair behind her ear. His knuckles ran lightly along her jawline. "I'm sorry. I guess I was annoyed when I thought I was going to have to break through that wall again."

"I think you've demolished it rather effectively, but

I did suspect for a minute that you might be punishing me for my aunt's obvious matchmaking attempts."

"Was she matchmaking?" he asked innocently.

Molly laughed. "You'd have to be blind not to notice. I don't think you're blind."

"She's a sweet lady."

"I know. That's what makes it so difficult. She'll have you hog-tied and bound for the altar in no time if you aren't careful."

He grinned. Then the grin faded, to be replaced by a frown. "She's done it before, hasn't she?" he asked in a low voice. "This Lee?"

"Yes, he's an old boyfriend." Lee Hayward was her aunt's foiled first attempt at matchmaking. Surprisingly, though, the bitterness Molly had felt against Lee in the past was now only dislike.

Rand didn't need further explanation. "Old, as in ex?" he prodded.

"Most definitely. I don't know why on earth Aunt Jo would have suggested contacting him, except to make you jealous."

"How serious was the thing with this Lee?" He said the name as though it left a bad taste in his mouth.

"It was a long time ago. If she'd asked me first, I could have told her that he wasn't the type to—"

"To what?"

To take on the responsibility of a ready-made family, she answered silently. She didn't want to remember the pain she'd felt when Lee made that clear. She had thought for a while that she was in love with him, but his callous words had killed the feeling quickly enough. He didn't intend to wait around until her aunt died, he'd told her, and he didn't enjoy the frequent dinners that the three of them shared. Afterward she'd realized with some relief that she been mistaken in her feelings. Luckily their relationship had never gone beyond the superficial.

Her gaze dropped to Rand's mouth. She wet her lips, letting her yearning show, and thought he made some kind of sound in his throat, but he didn't move. "You said you were going to kiss me," she whispered, lifting her parted lips in invitation.

"And you want me to?"

Her eyes flew to his, then fell when she saw the demand there. "Yes."

He took a deep breath before his mouth brushed gently over hers, then came back with slightly firmer pressure. His tongue dipped into the corner of her mouth, slid across her lower lip. Then he opened his lips wider to take a mock bite, barely touching.

His touch stole her breath. Her hand curled into a fist against his chest, then reached up to the back of his neck to pull his head down.

He was not to be rushed, though, and resisted the pressure of her hand. By slow degrees he deepened the kiss, his tongue making moist, lazy forays, then withdrawing. It wasn't so much a kiss as it was an introduction to the world of pure and absolute feeling.

Her eyes drifted shut and her body relaxed. She simply let her senses float on the voluptuous waves of half-consciousness.

His forearm supported her head when her neck refused to. His other hand slid around her waist, pulling her toward him, but the gearshift got in the way. She felt its hard knob press into her stomach and whimpered, not in pain, but in impatience with the inanimate object that was keeping them apart.

His hand left her waist briefly to make some adjustment to his seat, then he lifted her in one abrupt movement across the barrier and onto his lap.

This was much better, Molly thought dazedly, and wound her arms around his neck. It was her last rational thought for a long time. She was caught in the most enchanted experience ever, more magical, more sensual even than the kiss he had given her the night before.

Rand impatiently stripped the scarf from her hair, letting the long curls spill over his arm and down her back. His fingers dove into the glorious mass, releasing the beguiling scent of wild flowers. He could hear the hammer-beat of his pulse in his ears. The kiss—which *had* started as a mild punishment, though not for Jo's matchmaking—was fast mushrooming out of control. His mouth moved over hers with hungry nips, then roamed, exploring the planes and hollows of her face, only to return again and again to her lips.

She tasted so damned good, he thought. He wanted her with an urgency that he knew he would have to curb. He had wanted her since he had first seen the wind whip her hair like a flowing banner, first noticed the long, beautiful legs beneath the hem of her skirt, first looked into those expressive eyes, grayed in reflection of the impending storm. His motive was, had been from that moment, not only lust, not only passion, but something more.

What that "something" was Rand refused to consider. Had not considered in many years, not since—

The memory brought him up short. He jerked his head up as though her lips had burned him. He was breathing heavily as he struggled against the desire burning nearly out of control. "We . . . you . . ." He had to clear his throat of a sudden obstruction. "A car isn't the best setting for what I want to do to you right now."

Molly lifted her heavy lids reluctantly. When she saw, from Rand's expression, the battle going on in him, she came back from the mesmeric stupor with a crash. She struggled to sit up in his arms and looked around. Good Lord! she thought. What had she done? Her hand went to her cheek and her eyes darted about frantically.

People were beginning to gather in front of the church across the street. It would not do for Molly Beddingfield to be seen necking in the front seat of this very conspicuous car. "Oh, dear. I'm afraid you're right," she murmured in dismay.

Rand grinned. If that grin was strained, she chose not to notice it. He lifted her effortlessly back into her seat. His hands lingered under her knees, her back, for a moment longer than necessary.

To cover her agitation Molly busied herself with straightening her skirt, smoothing her hair. One of her flat-heeled shoes had come off, and she fumbled around on the floor for it. With her heart drumming in her ears, she looked for her scarf and found it under his long legs. She retrieved it, too, but when she would have tied her hair back again, he stopped her.

"Please, don't," he said huskily. "I love your hair wild and free like that."

She nodded and let her gaze fall to her lap.

With two fingers he turned her chin until she was facing him. "I would never hurt you, Molly," he said in a low voice. "In return let's promise each other that we won't play games. We both know it's happening too fast, but we may as well face what's between us. Since the moment we looked into each other's eyes for the first time, we've both known that this was special."

"Maybe," she answered.

"You're a stubborn lady." His smile took the bite out of the words.

Maybe she knew better than he did how special this was, she amended silently. She had lived long with her dream.

They drove along the back roads of the ocean-front properties, looking for and occasionally finding a For Sale sign, but by two o'clock nothing had stirred any particular interest in Rand. "What about your old friend in the real estate business?" he asked. "Would he be adverse to a call on Sunday?"

Molly's chin came up. "As a matter of fact, Aunt Jo telephoned him this morning," she said. "Just to see if he would be available today."

Rand grinned at her discomfort. "And would he?"

"Most certainly. Business always comes first with Lee. He said he'd be home all afternoon."

Rand decided he had made a strategic mistake, but jealousy had never been one of his failings. He was certain that seeing Molly in the presence of an old flame wouldn't bother him at all. "Then why don't we have lunch?" he suggested. "We can call from the restaurant and set up a time and place to meet him."

"Fine," Molly agreed calmly. "You can drop me off at home. If you have an agent you don't need me." Time away from Rand was what she needed, she thought. Distance, objectivity. The tension in the car had been palpable, despite the effort on both their parts to keep the conversation casual and light. And she certainly didn't want to spend any time with Lee.

He reached across the seat for her hand. "Molly."

"Yes?"

"You never did answer when I asked how serious it was with Lee. Is he still important to you?" Rand waited for her answer with narrowed eyes. He noted with surprise that he could feel jealousy, or something pretty damn close, after all.

Molly smiled, delighted at his expression of distaste. She decided to push a little further. "Not a bit. I just wish Aunt Jo didn't think I'm a poor wallflower who never gets to go anywhere."

He threw back his head and roared with unrestrained laughter. "Oh, honey," he said when he could speak again. "I guarantee no man would ever get that impression. But wait until you meet my mother!"

She looked at him in surprise. "I've met your mother," she reminded him. "She's charming."

His gaze swung to her. "That's right, you have. But you've never met her when I'm around. She turns into a dragon, trapping every female within miles to introduce to her impossible bachelor son." He chuckled again. "I remember one night last summer, I was home on leave and went to a party with her and Dad. She practically had a date arranged for me with the most gorgeous woman. . . ." He let his voice trail off suggestively.

She wouldn't ask. She wouldn't. "And . . .?" she said.

"And the woman was married and had three children." He shook his head. "Poor Mom." He lifted an arrogant brow. "Still, it was a terrible waste."

Rand never did get around to calling the real estate agent. The afternoon was too perfect with just the two of them. They walked the long, lonely beach, hands linked loosely, and talked.

After a while Rand spotted a depression in the dunes and led her there. Shaded by sea grasses, the niche was cozy, away from the wind, like a small cave looking out over the sea. Molly settled comfortably under his arm as though she had been made to fit there.

"Are you cold?" he asked, looking at her legs stretched out beside his, her ankles crossed, her small feet in the low-heeled shoes.

"Not now," she answered with a smile, cuddling in closer under his arm. "You're better than a blanket."

As they talked Rand had discovered that Molly was not fooling about her interest in the sea. Her knowledge of maritime history astounded him, and he told her so now. "I'm not sure that even my grandfather knew as much."

"I had a reason for learning so much about it."

"What's the reason?"

"It's personal," she answered, hedging. "I've never told anyone before."

"Great. I love being in on the ground floor of a secret."

"You'll laugh."

"You're a rear admiral in drag."

She giggled, and the sound was so startlingly incongruous to her ears that she giggled again.

"C'mon, honey, tell me," he urged, giving her a hard hug. "I promise not to laugh."

She looked up into those amused blue eyes, wondering if she could trust him. "I'm a closet romantic," she blurted out.

He grinned but didn't laugh, and his eyes were still puzzled. "So?"

She took a deep breath and drew her knees up to wrap her arms around them. Her eyes were fixed on the sea as she continued. "When I was a little girl I used to fantasize that someday a handsome seafaring hero would come sailing into port and sweep me away onto his ship. Sometimes it was a pirate ship, a four-masted schooner, sometimes it was a yacht, sometimes just a speedboat, but I tried to learn everything about ships so that when my hero came I would be prepared." She turned her head to look at Rand. "It sounds silly, I know, but in my scenario he and I would go sailing across the waves together. I never quite got beyond the fade-out," she finished blithely.

Rand looked stunned for a minute; then the laughter broke through. It rumbled up from his broad chest like an erupting volcano, shaking his whole body. "And I'm . . ." He gasped. "I'm in the Navy!"

Molly's whole body stiffened. "I didn't mean that. Damn you! What makes you think you qualify for my hero? You said you wouldn't laugh." She shrugged off his hold with a violent twist of her body and stumbled to her feet. "Damn you, Rand Eriksson!" she yelled.

"No! Come back here!" he shouted between whoops. He made a desperate lunge for her and grabbed her ankle, bringing her down onto the hard sand.

She fought him all the way, trying to dislodge his fingers with her other foot, but gradually, hand over hand, he brought her back into the shelter of their niche. "No, no, honey. Molly! Quiet down, sweetheart. Listen to me."

Molly didn't have a chance against Rand's superior strength, but she gave him a battle. Finally he pulled her against his chest, pinning her arms to her sides. "Honey, please. Listen to me."

Her hands worked ineffectually to loosen his grip. "Why should I?" she snapped, scraping her nails painfully across his hand.

"Ouch, dammit! Because, you little devil, I have known you just under two days and I'm crazy about you—and not too damned happy about it!"

Suddenly she went limp and quiet. Her beautiful blue-gray eyes were wide, their expression vulnerable. "You couldn't be," she whispered.

"And I'll never be able to fulfill your fantasies," he admitted ruefully.

She stiffened again. "You're married!" she accused.

"Hell, no! I'm not married. I'm a pilot!"

Her jaw went lax. "A wha-at?"

"A United States Navy pilot. I fly airplanes." When

she continued to look blank he added, "You know"—he released one arm to flatten his hand in the air—"*yeeough*." His hand dipped and dived with the sound effect. He grinned sheepishly. "I get seasick on boats."

Molly stared at him. "Ships," she corrected automatically. Her thoughts were whirling wildly. It was impossible. He said he was crazy about her and he got seasick. "But your father . . . your grandfather . . ." Men of the sea, both of them.

He shrugged. "I'm a throwback, and a great disappointment to them. I really tried to sail when I was a kid, but I thought I would die! They finally realized that it wasn't all in my head. When I was sixteen I started sneaking off to the local airport to take flying lessons. My father gave up for good when I graduated from college with a degree in aeronautical engineering."

"I can't believe it!" She laughed and shook her head.

"Do you think you could possibly alter your fantasies, darling, to let the handsome hero swoop down out of the sky?" he asked in a low voice as he smoothed her tumbled hair away from her face. "Because I'd very much like to be your hero."

She searched his eyes for a sign of mockery, but there was none. "I'll work on it," she murmured.

"You do that," he said with an outrageous grin. "I promise to do everything I can to help."

Resolute in his exploration of her mouth, his lips were firm, cool at first, but almost instantly grew hot and sultry with desire. With the audacity of his ancient ancestors, he traced the soft underside of her upper lip, her smooth, even teeth, the velvet roughness of her tongue, until her senses were spinning out of control like a star gone awry on its axis. She curled her fingers into the warm, soft wool of his sweater.

Rand was powerless to control the lightning-fast response of his body when she moved so enticingly against him. With a twist of his body he laid her back. He looked down into her face, her lips moist and delectable, her thick lashes fanning her cheeks with half-circles of shadow. He knew he could take her here, now, in the sand, in broad daylight. His need to be inside her warmth grew swiftly to an unexpected craving that ate at him like an animal snarling in his loins. This helpless physical desperation was totally foreign to him. He had always been master of his sexual appetites, until now, until Molly. With her, those appetites threatened to rage out of control. He could no more draw away from this delightful armful of femininity than he could will his heart to stop beating.

He heard his own breath, ragged and labored, as his mouth explored her face, then came back to her moist lips to drink deeply from her honeyed nectar. Just one more kiss, he told himself, then he'd stop.

His hand slid beneath her bulky sweater to find her, and a groan escaped him. He heard it wonderingly, and then forgot everything when he felt the sweet peak of her breast thrust forward through its covering of lace into his palm.

One of her smooth hands dipped into the collar of his shirt, her nails scraping lightly down his spine. An explosive shudder ripped through his body, taking him by surprise. Shaken, he wrenched his mouth from hers to bury his lips in the soft skin of her neck, breathing hard to relieve the pain in his starved lungs.

She shifted slightly. He tightened his arms to prevent her from making any further movement.

She whispered something—his name?—and he shushed her. "No . . . darling, please . . . give me a minute," he murmured.

He withdrew his hand reluctantly from her breast and smoothed down the sweater, slowly, as if it were the most important thing in the world to get the garment exactly where it should be. Finally he raised his head to look at her—her thickly-lashed lids now lifted to reveal the smoky desire in her eyes, her wild hair—through a blur of want, of need. His eyes fixed on her swollen lips. "Oh, Lord. Did I hurt you, Molly?"

She looked up to see his head crowned by the waving grasses on the dune above them; the sky beyond, the same arresting color as his eyes. She raised her hand to his cheek in a comforting caress. "No," she said shakily, and sighed. Her response to the embrace had been every bit as violent as his. She couldn't let him take all the responsibility for such a magnificent, if slightly rough, experience. After all, she was not a fragile piece of porcelain.

Today, with this man, she was for the first time the woman he had challenged her to be, and she gloried in the feeling. She smiled, and though she wasn't aware that the change in her showed so clearly, it was evident in that smile. "You didn't hurt me," she said. "I'm a grown woman, Rand."

Rationality finally pierced the frustration in Rand's eyes, but it was slightly clouded by doubt. He lifted his gaze to the horizon, watching the waves sigh against the shore, then looked back at her. "You said that you never went beyond the fade-out. Does that mean that you're a virgin, Molly?" he asked hesitantly. Asked, but didn't really expect the answer she gave.

"Yes, I am."

He was startled, but she met his gaze calmly. "And I don't intend to apologize for it. I'm not saving myself, or anything like that, but I am rather choosy. And there were reasons." She gave a small shrug. "So far there hasn't been anyone I wanted badly enough."

Rand held his breath, astonished at the thrill of pleasure that shot through him at the realization that no one had ever touched her in the way of a man and a woman. Then he immediately and determinedly set the thought aside. Good Lord, what had happened to him? Virgins had always been an anathema, dangerous, and to be avoided like the plague. Molly inspired feelings that he didn't know he was capable of, possessive, protective feelings that she probably wouldn't thank him for. She was a very independent lady, his Molly. His Molly—he liked that. "Do you mind if I ask what the reasons were?" he said.

She squirmed a little, but didn't fight hard for her freedom. "Yes, I do mind. It's none of your business."

"Don't get mad. The kiss we just shared makes it my business," he said gently. "That was no ordinary kiss. None of them have been. Those were the kind of kisses that lead to more, as you know full well. There's passion in you, honey."

She stared at him. Then she was the one to turn

her head, to seek the horizon with her gaze. "When I entered college," she finally said, "I suppose I went with the idea that I would learn more than maritime history. I thought I would probably . . . Rand, could we please sit up?"

He rolled aside, maneuvering them until he was half-sitting, his back against a bank of sand. He kept her between his bent knees, his arms loosely holding her. "But you didn't," he said.

It wasn't a question, but she answered anyway. "No." She leaned forward, pulling away from the haven of his arms.

He released her, letting his forearms rest on his knees and his hands dangle, providing a harbor, should she need one, but not shackling her.

"I've never told this to anyone," she said. "Even Aunt Jo doesn't know."

The smooth curve of her throat, her delicate profile, were backlighted by the reflection of the sun on the sand. She was quiet, staring out over the ocean for a long moment, but Rand didn't prod. It appeared that she was about to open up to him, maybe to reveal some of the things that made her such an intriguing woman.

Her voice, when she continued, held sorrow in its husky tones. "My sister—it doesn't matter which one—found out that she was pregnant, during her sophomore year in college. She didn't tell anyone until after she had the abortion."

Molly shuddered, and now Rand did put his hand on her shoulder, bringing her unresisting body back against him. The story was difficult for her, he could tell that. "I'm sure she was young and scared," he said.

Molly squeezed her eyes shut, grateful for the comfort of his arm and the words. "Yes," she whispered. "She was . . . but afterward . . . there was a tragic complication. She developed an infection and now she can't have children at all. The irony of it is that she married the father. They adore each other, but they share the grief every day."

He could almost taste the pain in her voice, and he ached with her.

"They've tried to adopt," she went on, "but babies are scarce and waiting lists are long. It may be years before a child becomes available."

"Honey, science has come a long way with birth control," he said gently. He was relieved to see the acidic glance she gave him.

"I know about birth control pills," she said shortly. "That isn't why I'm a virgin."

"Go on."

"My sister almost died. The clinic called me—she had put me down as her next of kin. I had to lie to Aunt Jo to get away. I sat by her bedside for three days and listened to her delirious ramblings, and I was stunned by the things I heard. The beautiful sister whom I'd always envied had evidently been hopping from bed to bed for years, ever since she was younger than I was then. She kept saying over and over that she was empty, empty. . . ." Molly's voice trailed off, and she blinked at the tears that blurred her eyes. "I knew right then that I couldn't handle such a life. So I decided that I would wait for someone who could fill my empty places before I made love."

She shrugged off the melancholy. "I just haven't found such a man."

The primitive urge that he had felt the first time he met her, the temptation to sweep this lovely lady off her feet, was suddenly even stronger in Rand. Could he put aside the past? He'd thought of permanence, a wife and family, but not often and not lately. Could he let himself care . . . enough? He had a track record that made the idea highly improbable. But then, he'd never known any woman like this one, either. "Molly, we have to talk about this."

She twisted to face him, her hand covering his lips to halt any more words. "Rand, I want you to know right from the start, whatever happens, no commitment, no chains, no ties," she said softly, as though she had seen into his mind. "I'm not interested in permanency either. I have too many responsibilities of my own."

He was stunned. What was she saying? *He* was the one who had always avoided commitment as adroitly as a broken field runner, but her response left him feeling as if the earth had dropped from beneath him. Contrarily, he started to argue the point. "But I want . . ." He stopped. What did he want?

Her fingers trembled slightly against his skin. "Let's give ourselves more time. If we decide to make love, we will both go into a relationship with our eyes open and our individualities intact."

He stared at her for a long moment, delving into the depths of her eyes, trying to read her thoughts, but they were not open to him. He wanted her as he had never wanted another woman, and his deeper emotions were in a turmoil. He sighed and rose to his feet, pulling her up beside him. "Okay. For now. Hell, let's go pack!"

Five

The move was accomplished easily and quickly, and by sundown all of Rand's things were arranged and unpacked in the master bedroom on the first floor.

Aunt Jo was buoyant with enthusiasm at dinner that night. Watching her aunt pass the chicken to Rand for the third time, Molly wondered fondly if Aunt Jo had doubled her nightly ration of one ounce of bourbon or if her eagerness was caused by the simple pleasure of having a man in the house again.

If that were the case, Molly could easily understand. She'd felt it, too, the vibrancy in the atmosphere, different sounds—bass now in harmony with soprano—different scents, male scents of outdoors and after-shave and leather mingling with delicate floral perfumes. The entire mood in the house was different, and utterly exciting. But Molly knew she and Aunt Jo were reacting to Rand's presence in different ways. Aunt Jo was in hog heaven, while Molly's mind was filled with misgivings.

"Thank you, ma'am," Rand said, holding up a hand when Aunt Jo offered him another serving of apple pie. "But I've had all I can hold for now."

I should think so, Molly said to herself.

Aunt Jo replaced the plate on the trivet and sighed, rather dramatically, Molly thought. "It is so nice to have a man in the house again, Rand," she said pleasantly, echoing Molly's thoughts. "Molly and I do very well alone, but there's just something about a masculine presence that makes one feel . . . secure."

Molly scarcely paid attention to what Aunt Jo was saying. She was admiring Rand instead. He had changed for dinner. He was wearing a blue blazer over buff-colored slacks and a pale blue shirt that made his eyes look as dark as midnight in comparison. A tan-and-navy-striped silk tie was knotted neatly at his neck.

She watched as he hooked one arm over the back of his chair and looked thoughtfully at Aunt Jo. The action parted his jacket, giving Molly, seated at his right, a throat-drying view of his powerful chest, his flat belly. Just the sight of him stirred filaments of desire that shocked her with their strength. He was so . . . so male! How was she going to survive the next two weeks without making a complete fool of herself?

By acting just as you've always acted, she answered her own question sternly. By listening to the conversation around you instead of going off into some dreamy world where your imagination leads you astray. Like now. She forced her attention from the disturbing man.

Rand hadn't noticed Molly's reaction to him because he was trying to concentrate on what Jo was saying. His thoughts, however, kept tending to settle instead on the woman to his right. If he stretched his fingers an inch or two, they could touch her hand, which rested lightly on the table.

Rand turned his own hand into a loose fist and stared down at it, trying to analyze his contrary reaction to Molly's pronouncement that afternoon. He had never had a problem being honest with himself. It was a trait that was a necessity for a pilot. When you were up there, in the sky, when there was no one else to rely on except yourself, you had better not be less than honest. He knew his own failings and recognized his strengths, so why was his evaluation of this particular situation difficult? Maybe it was because he didn't want to ask himself some of the questions that had to be asked.

For instance, was he so hell-bent on having Molly because she had unknowingly made herself a challenge by her firm avowal that there would be no permanent ties between them? He looked at the question from all angles, and decided that the answer was no.

Though it hadn't happened often enough to destroy his ego, women had said no to him before. He had never felt compelled to overcome their objections. But the situation with Molly was different, he admitted. She hadn't said no to the physical aspect of their relationship—indeed, she had left that door wide open—only to the idea of permanency. So why wasn't he delighted?

That was the second question.

He had known Molly less than two days, certainly not long enough to want to marry her. There. The word was out. He turned it over in his mind. Absurd.

A sigh escaped him, earning him a sharp look from Jo Beddingfield, and he cursed his rudeness. She was a spunky lady, and he liked her very much. "I'm sorry," he said quickly. "Please forgive me for letting my mind wander. I . . . uh . . . forgot to let the base know that I've moved." And what would the base care? He was on leave. "Have you had security problems before?" he asked, returning to the subject of a minute ago.

"One or two, nothing serious," Jo answered, her manner indicating that they were very serious indeed.

Molly decided that she couldn't let this go on any longer. Her aunt was going to let the poor man think they lived on the very brink of danger. "One peeping Tom, aged twelve," she said, "and one drunk who slept it off on the front porch. We didn't even know that he was there until the next morning. The police chief is a friend of Aunt Jo's, and now the officers on the beat check the house regularly."

Jo ignored the rebuke in Molly's voice. "I'll put the leftover chicken in the refrigerator, Rand. You might be hungry for a midnight snack." She rose and went into the kitchen.

Had Aunt Jo really simpered? Molly wondered, astonished. Yes, that was *definitely* a simper. She met Rand's grin with a wry smile.

"Let's have our coffee in the living room," Aunt Jo said as she returned. "Rand, would you help Molly with the tray?"

"Sure."

The silver tray was prepared, and transferring the coffee from the percolator to the fluted pot was all that remained to be done. Rand walked into the kitchen behind Molly, standing close, but not touching. The lack of physical contact was no impediment to his power over her libido, though. The warmth from his body reached out to encircle her in an embrace that was just as effective as the security of his arms.

She glanced over her shoulders to see the sparkle in his eyes, and forgot all her good intentions. A feeling bordering on contentment filled her, surprising her. Content was the last way she'd expect to feel around this man, and the last thing she needed. She didn't want to become too comfortable in his presence, she told herself, and then wondered whom she thought she was kidding.

Her frown must have indicated her reservations, for Rand took her firmly by the shoulders. Turning her to face him, he studied the expression in her eyes for a long moment. Then his finger smoothed away the tiny line between her brows. "Don't," he said softly, then touched his lips to hers.

She didn't respond.

"Molly? What's wrong?"

"Nothing." She pulled out of his arms and deliberately lightened the tone of her voice. "We'd better go in, or Aunt Jo'll wonder what we're doing out here."

He reached around her for the tray, leaving a quick, burning kiss at the side of her neck on the way. "Well, if she wants me to compromise you, she'll have my complete cooperation."

Right now it was a joke to Rand, Molly knew. She couldn't tell him all of her suspicions, that Aunt Jo was settling him in for the duration, that the older woman had decided that he might "do" for her niece. As Molly had told him, this was not the first time Aunt Jo had played matchmaker, but with Lee her efforts hadn't been quite so obvious. Molly felt a panicky catch in her throat as she pushed through the swinging door and held it open for Rand. She didn't want to be embarrassed in front of this man. She was definitely going to have to have a talk with her aunt.

"By the way," he said as they walked to the living room, "there's a dance at the Officers' Club in Oceana Saturday night. Would you like to go?"

"What a lovely idea," Aunt Jo answered for Molly. "You'll have to splurge on a new dress, Molly."

Molly gave her aunt a knowing look. "I imagine I can find something in my closet," she told her. Then she smiled at Rand. "Thank you, I'd love to go."

Her aunt's chin took on a stubborn tilt. "You must get a new dress, and I don't want to hear another word about it."

They glared at each other, and Rand looked interested, but neither of them enlightened him.

"Did you have any luck with your house-hunting this afternoon?" Aunt Jo asked when they had all been served. "Did you see Lee?"

"It might take more than one day, Aunt Jo," Molly said dryly. "And we didn't call Lee."

"You didn't?"

Aunt Jo didn't sound surprised, and Molly wished the kisses she and Rand had shared on the beach hadn't left such a visible mark on her. "Rand wanted to see all the neighborhoods before he decides where he wants to live."

Aunt Jo nodded. "I can understand that. Personally I prefer the Bay Colony area."

"Rand is looking for ocean-front property, Aunt Jo."

"Oh, yes. That's right." Aunt Jo frowned and touched her temple with a finger, a sure sign that she was trying to recover a stray memory.

"Have you thought of something?" Molly asked, then explained to Rand, "Aunt Jo's customers often know who is moving or selling almost before the people themselves do. And often the prices are much more reasonable on property found that way. Have you thought of something, Aunt Jo?"

"What? Oh, no. I was . . . No, it's not important." Aunt Jo stood, and said briskly, "I think I'll have an early evening. I'm rather tired, dear, would you see to the cleaning up?"

"Aunt Jo," Molly chided, "you haven't finished your coffee."

"Coffee might keep me awake."

It never had before, thought Molly, but she didn't argue. "Good night."

Rand got to his feet and leaned down to leave a kiss on the weathered cheek. As she left the room he called, "Good night, Aunt Jo."

Her aunt loved that.

Rand cleared his throat and sat down again. "You and your aunt seem to have a difference of opinion about your dress for Saturday night. Is there a problem?"

Molly laughed, a slightly husky sound. "Well, you

see, I have these three older sisters, none of whom could bear to wear a garment in its second season. So I inherit the hand-me-downs. I'm really quite lucky. I have a closet stuffed with clothes. For some reason Aunt Jo has begun to badger me lately, almost as though she resents it."

"And you don't?"

"Heavens, no." Her gaze dropped to her cup. "At least, I don't think so. I used to envy their beauty and resent their freedom a bit, but I hope I've outgrown that. And I never resented all the gorgeous clothes I got from them," she said with finality.

Molly seemed to want the subject dropped, so Rand replied with a simple nod. But she had revealed more to him by her expression than she realized. Though her tone was light, she hadn't quite been able to keep a slight bitterness from showing in her eyes. In spite of her denial, he wondered at her relationship with her sisters. He had never had to stand in the shadow of anyone else. What would it be like to be compared constantly to another? he wondered.

They sipped their coffee in silence, both conscious of the noises coming from upstairs—water running, closet door opening and closing, padding footsteps.

The electricity between them sparked each time their eyes met, so they avoided looking at each other. Still, Molly knew that she didn't have to look at Rand to be totally aware of the vitality that radiated from him. His masculinity seemed to enter her pores from every angle, filling her with the heat of anticipation.

Finally all was quiet except for the crackle of flames from the fireplace and the delicate clink of coffee cups as they were returned to saucers.

Molly sighed, and was startled at how loud the sound was. "Well, I don't suppose the dishes are going to do themselves," she said. She set her cup on the tray and started to lift it, when Rand's hand stopped her.

"I'll get that."

"You don't have to help," she said, her hostess face firmly in place. "Just sit here and finish your coffee."

"Hey," he said gently. "I thought we were beyond this. If I didn't want to help you I wouldn't have offered."

Her gaze touched his briefly, hesitated, and slid away. Memories of their first meeting surfaced, when all she'd had to keep her together was silly platitudes. This man had shaken her out of her safe rut with a vengeance. No, she didn't want to go back to being the snippy little prude she was then. On the other hand, she wasn't moving as fast as Rand was in this relationship. She straightened and ran distracted fingers through her fiery mane. Why was she letting the situation get to her like this? She shook off the feelings of unease and smiled, hoping her face didn't look as stiff as it felt.

"All right," she said. "If you'll bring in the tray, I'll be gracious and let you do the dishes too. I should warn you, though, we do them the old-fashioned way, by hand."

His soft chuckle roused the nerve endings in her spine. "Do you think I wouldn't know how?"

She hesitated, eyeing his large frame as he rose, stretching a little, and picked up the tray as though the heavy silver weighed nothing at all. He lifted an enquiring brow.

"You've probably washed a few dishes, but I doubt that you make it a habit." She started to add something, but stopped, catching her lower lip between her teeth.

"Go on," he urged softly, the roguish dimple playing in his cheek.

"The first time I saw you I thought that a woman might domesticate you a bit, but she would never tame you."

Rand caught his breath, unaware that his lips had curved into an enigmatic half-smile. Talk about hitting the nail on the head, he thought. Yet the idea was growing, feeding on her presence, that if anyone *could* tame him, it would be Molly Beddingfield.

He waited until she was up to her elbows in dishwashing detergent before he started in on her again. "I owe you an apology, Molly," he said.

"For what?"

"Yesterday, at the reception . . ."

Had it only been yesterday? she thought in shock.

"I said some things that I shouldn't have. Made some harsh judgments about you. I'm sorry."

Her heart melted as she glanced at him. His expression was very sober, like that of a young boy with a duty to perform that he was determined to put behind him. She smiled gently. "That's all right, Rand. I understand."

"I have no excuse for my behavior." The fork and dish towel in his hands were forgotten as he propped one hip against the counter. His gaze met hers. "Except that I haven't met a woman like you before."

Lifting a saucepan from the sudsy water, she rinsed it carefully under the flow from the faucet. Her movements were slow and deliberate, giving her time to think. At last she placed the pan in the rack to drain. "I should apologize too. I wasn't myself at the reception. I acted like a snob."

He made a demurring sound, but she ignored it. "Yes, I did." She gave the dishcloth an extrahard twist and shook it out to hang it over the arm of the faucet. A small bottle of hand lotion sat on the edge of the sink. She poured a drop into her palm and massaged it into her skin. "Do you want more coffee before I wash the pot?" she asked.

Rand wasn't about to say no. "Sure, if you'll have some with me." He finished drying the saucepan while she got down mugs from a cabinet and poured the coffee. She took the mugs to the kitchen table and sat down. He felt a moment's compassion as he took the chair at a right angle to hers and waited for her to continue. She looked serious and a little disturbed.

Her hands curved around the mug to absorb its warmth. "Sometimes I feel like I have one foot stuck in yesterday," she said. "I love my career, and history; but occasionally I need someone to remind me—as you said—that this is the twentieth century."

Rand slid his coffee mug out of his way and reached for her hand. The scent of roses filled his senses as he lifted her fingers to his lips. He turned her hand over and kissed the palm. "Only one foot, Molly Beddingfield. In many ways you are very much a woman of today," he murmured, meeting her eyes with a glow in his own that he didn't even try to camouflage.

Her smile was slow in coming, but it lit her entire

face. "Thank you, Rand. That's a very nice compliment, coming from a man who knows better."

With a smooth movement he leaned over to pluck her from her chair, and she found herself sitting on his lap, cradled closely against his broad chest. He caught her chin between his thumb and fingers and tilted her face up. "I mean it, Molly. When I first looked at you, what I saw was a vibrant woman whose hair was a wild incitement to fire any man's blood. You wore tailored clothes, but your body strained to be free of them. And the way you move . . . Oh, Molly, the way you move is the most exciting thing I've ever seen. You're lovely, Molly. Unbelievably feminine and very appealing . . ." He chuckled. "I would add 'sexy as hell,' but you're beginning to get that stunned look in your eyes and I'm afraid you'll slap my face."

"I won't slap your face," she promised, and he went on.

"There's passion in you, honey, and it shows. You may try to disguise it, but it is definitely there. I would very much like to be the one to awaken that passion in you. Tell me, do I fill your empty places?" He asked the question huskily, just before his mouth took hers, his tongue sinking into her honeyed warmth, leaving her no chance to answer.

Small ribbons of fire instantly curled upward from the core of her desire to tangle with the nerve endings throughout her body. Dangerous or not, she had wanted this all evening. She twisted slightly so that she could wind her arms around his neck. Her shifting provoked a groan from deep within his throat, and the hand at her hip pressed her closer, into the hard heat of his arousal.

Oh, yes, there was passion in her, thought Molly, a passion that surpassed anything she could have imagined. Her eyes drifted shut, closing off one sense so that she could revel in the others. His mouth tasted like strong black coffee, his shoulders felt like a powerful mountain as her hands explored. Then her fingers dove into his hair, urging him to deepen the kiss.

Instead he dragged his lips painfully from hers, burying his face in the curve of her neck. His breathing was rapid, its rhythm erratic. His hand left her hip and moved upward to her rib cage, where it paused before moving on almost helplessly to cover her breast. His fingers kneaded gently, until she arched her back, thrusting herself into his hand, blindly asking for a firmer touch.

The tumultuous excitement building between them suddenly exploded. His mouth sought hers again, this time demanding and hungry, and expectant. When he drew back to fill his starving lungs with air, the rasping sound echoed her own breathing.

"Molly, look at me," he commanded hoarsely.

Her lids were so heavy that it was an effort to raise them, but finally she managed. Rand's blue eyes blazed down at her with a depth of desire she'd never seen in a man before, a ferocity that made her swallow hard.

"I want you, you know that," he said. "I want you now. Can we go to my room?"

Suddenly Molly realized where they were. She sat up slowly, painfully. "We can't, not here," she said in a voice so weak with desire that she hardly recognized it as her own.

He sighed and rested his forehead against hers. "I was afraid you'd say that."

"Oh, Rand," she breathed. "I'm sorry. But if Aunt Jo came down . . ."

He smoothed the length of her hair with a trembling hand. "I know, honey. I know. Believe it or not I have some scruples myself about making love to you in your aunt's house. Damn, I should have kept that motel room."

Frustration curved his lips into a parody of a smile, and she put her fingers over them, offering comfort. "I really am sorry. You must think I'm deliberately teasing you."

He shook his head and eased her off his lap. When they were standing close but not touching, he took another deep breath, one he hoped would be calming, and shoved his hands into his pockets. "No, I don't think you're a tease. It's more my fault than yours." He turned away, impatiently raking his hand through his hair, then swung back. "I know that I'm rushing things. I also know that this wasn't the time or place, but you should understand that, should we find ourselves in the right place at the right time, I will make love to you. I want you desperately."

She still was not free of his spell. Gravity or some other law of nature drew her toward his magnetic body. She swayed until he caught her by the shoulders. "Molly . . ." he growled dangerously.

Her head fell forward as though too heavy for her neck.

"Molly," he repeated, a trace of panic in his voice.

What was she doing? she asked herself, beginning to feel panicked too. "I'd better go upstairs," she said.

"That's the most sensible idea you've had all night."

At noon on Monday Rand met her on the beach in front of the Maritime Museum with a picnic basket from a well-known gourmet shop a couple of blocks away. That night they drove into Norfolk to wander through the shops of Waterside, a development on the bay. Hands entwined, heads close, they strolled along the embankment in the moonlight.

On Tuesday evening they ate hamburgers at a fast-food place and went to see the latest of the Star Trek adventure movies, dragging along a protesting Aunt Jo. Rand admitted to a secret yearning to fly to the stars. Jo confessed to thinking that Dr. Spock was very sexy. Molly agreed, earning herself a very good imitation of a punishing kiss. The kiss caught her by surprise, and she glanced at her aunt, but Jo was beaming. Naturally.

Wednesday night they left Jo and Milton arguing amiably over a game of Scrabble and attended an exhibit of primitive African art at the Chrysler Museum. Rand kept Molly laughing with his lewd comments on the fertility goddesses.

When Rand escorted Molly home from work on Thursday, Aunt Jo met them at the door. "Here you are," she said cheerfully, and unnecessarily.

Rand's eyes met Molly's in a secret smile. "Yes," he agreed. "Here we are."

The older woman was blocking the door, so the two of them stood patiently waiting for her to move. "Well, come in," Aunt Jo ordered, ignoring the fact that she was standing in their way. "Dinner's almost ready."

She turned, and they meekly followed her. "Did you find a dress?"

"Yes, I did," Molly said, shaking her head in exasperated affection. "I went shopping on my lunch hour. You didn't have to send Rand to check up on me." He had arrived as the museum was closing, to greet her with a tender kiss and deliver a message from her aunt that she was not to come home without a new dress. Agatha had loved it—and him. Judging by the glimmer of curiosity in her secretary's gaze, Molly knew that she would be badgered with questions the next day.

"Today's Thursday," Aunt Jo said in defense. "Someone had to push you. Well? Where is it?"

"It's being altered," Molly said, then firmly changed the subject. "Do you need any help with dinner?"

Their dinner conversation was light and trivial, and over desert Molly asked Rand if he had seen any promising houses.

He shook his head. "Not a one, but I did finally call your friend, the real estate agent. He's out of town until Monday."

Molly grinned at his grumbling. "He'll have something to show you. Lee is really a good agent."

Aunt Jo looked from one of them to the other before throwing out casually, "You could buy this place, Rand. We're not right on the beach and it's a bit of a barn, but from the upstairs windows we have a lovely view of the ocean."

Molly swallowed a bite of apple pie whole. Her jaw dropped in astonishment. "Buy th—" she mouthed, but no sound emerged from her throat.

"I think I'd be better off with something slightly

smaller." Rand grinned. "How many bedrooms does your house have?"

"Nine if you include the servant's quarters on the third floor," Aunt Jo said. "We never go up there anymore."

"Buy *this* place," Molly repeated in a strangled whisper. "This is the family home. You've always told me we'd never sell."

"Ah, well . . . I know I said that. But I've been thinking lately that a smaller place might be nice, easier to take care of"—her eyes twinkled—"cheaper."

Molly was stunned into silence as she carefully laid down her fork and continued to stare at her aunt.

"I really don't know why Papa hung on to it for so long," Aunt Jo went on. "When the motels and shops started to move in so close, he should have sold."

"But what about Madeline and Louise and Michelle?" Molly asked.

"Madeline?" Rand repeated in a quiet voice. He was suddenly very still, but neither of the women seemed to notice. It couldn't be, he thought. There were millions of women named Madeline. But the connection . . . with his parents . . . ?

"My sisters," Molly answered him without taking her eyes off her aunt. "I told you about them. They're all married."

"I used to know a Madeline from around here," he said. "What's her married name?" he asked carefully.

"Bryant," said Molly distractedly. "Aunt Jo . . ."

Rand breathed again. His relief was so great that he slumped in his chair, until Jo said, "I thought it was Gibson. At least I know it isn't Conners. That was years ago."

"You're right," Molly said. "Bryant was husband number two." She flicked a glance of explanation to Rand. "Madeline goes through husbands as if they were peanuts."

Rand's heart hit his toes. Dear Lord, he thought. It was the same Madeline. "Do your sisters get home very often?" he asked.

"Never have time," said Aunt Jo with a sniff. "Or so they say. They're too involved in their busy lives."

He let out a sigh of deep relief and watched the continuing byplay between the two women with a certain amusement. Should he mention the coincidence casually? he wondered. In an offhand way? *Oh, by the way, I used to know a Madeline Conners.* Should he tell them both, or wait until he had Molly alone? His mind spun with the possibilities for disaster. He and Molly were poised on the threshold of a relationship that promised so much, so very much. He remembered the resentment in her eyes when she'd talked about living in the shadow of her sisters. He couldn't stand the thought of her withdrawing behind that wall of stiffness again, shutting him out. But that was exactly what would happen if he told her about Madeline.

He wasn't going to tell her at all, he decided suddenly. The Madeline he'd been so infatuated with all those years ago had been married to two husbands since then. She never came home, and if she did, the chances of her remembering him were virtually nil. He dismissed Madeline Bryant-Conners-whatever from his mind and let his gaze linger on Molly.

She hadn't changed her clothes before dinner. Clad in her tailored suit, she looked businesslike and unapproachable. He began to anticipate the hours ahead, when her aunt would retire upstairs, when he would strip off that severe jacket, pull the pins from her hair, and begin to kiss those beautiful lips. There was no memory in the universe that could compare with the reality of this vibrant woman.

He had enjoyed these last few days, spending time with Molly. They had talked a lot, sharing childhood memories, reminiscences, experiences, in a great hurry to get all the things said that had to be said. But underneath it all was a conflagration that burned hot, that threatened to break out and consume them both before the time was right. For they both knew that their relationship was moving at breakneck speed.

Those late hours together—when Jo had gone to bed, when the house was quiet—were a test of his control, but he eagerly endured the torture. The evenings always ended the only way they could, with the two of them saying good night at the foot of the stairs.

The truth was, he couldn't keep his hands off Molly. Touching her was a deep compulsion, one he couldn't begin to fight. He tried to keep the touching on an affectionate level—linking their fingers, throwing his arm lightly across her shoulders, a casual kiss. The ploy often didn't work. One taste of her lips, no matter how fleeting, one sniff of her fragrant skin, her hair, and he was flying high, as intoxicated as if he'd been drinking steadily of hundred-proof moonshine.

She shifted in her chair, and he caught a glimpse of the curve of her breast and remembered its weight in his hand. Forcing his attention back to the conversation, he shifted too. His movement didn't make him any more comfortable, though.

"Molly," Aunt Jo was saying firmly, "when I'm gone the house will be yours, and yours alone. The girls know that. I told them years ago, and they agreed. You were the one who stayed here to live with me, while they all went their own ways. You've given up the most."

"Aunt Jo, I told you—"

"I know." She waved away the denial. "You chose to stay. Still, you didn't have a choice, not really. You get the house, no argument, so you should have some say in its disposal. Do you want to sell?"

"I don't know." Molly's head was spinning wildly.

"It might help you to make up your mind if I tell you that the last offer I turned down was half a million. We could live pretty well on the interest. We wouldn't touch the principle, of course," Aunt Jo added primly.

"You could probably get more," inserted Rand.

"Half a million *dollars?*" Molly asked, choking. My Lord! she thought. That was five hundred one-thousand-dollar bills! That was—

"It was just a thought." Aunt Jo cut another generous slice of pie and put it on Rand's plate.

"I don't . . ." he began, but they both ignored him. He shrugged and picked up his fork.

Molly's spirits were sinking. Surely Aunt Jo was only rambling, she thought. Her aunt would never sell this house. She had vowed not to sell too often for Molly to take the thought seriously. "The dinner was delicious, Aunt Jo," she said quietly, earning herself a sharp look.

* * *

She should have stuck with black, Molly chided herself the following night as she revolved in front of her mirror. But she hadn't been able to resist the dress. Deep gold petals of chiffon were gathered at her waist and gradually grew lighter in color as they fanned out and up, reaching for her shoulders, leaving her arms bare and shaping a neckline that came to a point between her breasts. The same phenomenon of dark fading into light, of delicate layers that lifted on the slightest puff of air, swirled lovingly around her hips and fell to an irregular hemline below her knees.

It was Molly's dress. The golden hue would have faded to nothing against the blondeness of any of her sisters, but on her it accentuated golden highlights that she had never realized were hidden in the flames of her hair. Her skin glowed like a ripening apricot, and her eyes were smoky and dark.

She had brushed her hair until it crackled, then pulled one side back with a glittery comb and left the rest free and wild, the way Rand liked it.

Free and wild and a little barbaric was how she looked from head to toe, she thought, and wondered at her sanity. Her palms were damp, but she resisted the urge to wipe them on the dress. She picked up a bottle of perfume, a scent she'd never worn before, but that the salesperson had assured her would drive her man wild. Wild. There was that word again. She picked up a lightweight shawl and a gold evening purse and flipped out the light as she left the room.

Rand was waiting for her at the bottom of the

stairs. He looked tall even from this perspective, and handsome and utterly masculine in his dress uniform. His hair was combed neatly, the creases in his dark trousers were as straight as plumb lines, and the epaulets on the shoulders of his white mess jacket were squared perfectly, as was the black bow tie. His white hat, with its shiny black bill and gold braid, was tucked formally under his arm.

Molly paused, unconsciously waiting. Her lack of experience was definitely going to be a handicap tonight, she thought. In his uniform Rand possessed an added assurance, a cavalier self-confidence that threatened her own.

He turned and froze, his feet rooted to the spot. Only his eyes moved, traveling down the length of her, indulging in slow luxury the sight of the vision above him. Finally he moved, planting himself at the center of the bottom step, legs slightly apart. He took the hat in one hand and wordlessly held out the other toward her.

The heat in his eyes threatened to turn her knees to liquid. She descended carefully, almost hesitantly, until she reached the step that put her eyes on a level with his, and put her hand in his.

His fingers closed possessively around her hand, sending a further thrill up her bare spine. "You are beautiful," he said in a voice that was low and thick with emotion.

"Thank you." She smiled, and the smile seemed to relax both of them.

"Would I ruin your magnificence if I kissed you?"

She chuckled. "I hope not."

Very slowly he drew her into his arms. His head

dipped. She willed her eyelids to stay up so that she could revel in every nuance of his expression. The kiss was brief and light, like the brush of a feather, but warm and promising too. He drew back to study her expression with equal thoroughness, then laughed softly and settled his hat on her head, leaving both arms free to lift her off the step, twirling her in a half-circle against him. This kiss was much more thorough, sending her senses reeling as she clung to his broad shoulders.

"Well, well, all ready to go?" Aunt Jo's voice drifted into the hall.

Thank goodness Aunt Jo always began speaking before she entered a room, Molly thought as she tried to collect herself.

Rand let her toes touch the floor, but he didn't release her. His voice was still unsteady when he spoke.

"We're ready, but I'm not sure Molly should be let out in public, Jo. She might undermine our entire air defense force, looking the way she does tonight."

"Oh, my dear," breathed Aunt Jo, her eyes wide and unbelieving. "You are lovely."

"I must have really looked awful before, if this is the kind of reaction I'm getting with a new dress," Molly teased. She pulled out of Rand's arms and kissed her aunt's cheek. "We won't be late," she promised.

"Yes, we will," Rand countered. "Probably very late."

Light, music, and a brilliant red carpet spilled out of the entrance to the Oceana Officers' Club. A plane was parked in the grassy triangle formed by the two arms of the driveway. Long and dark, the plane looked like a sleek bullet poised for takeoff.

"Is that the kind of plane you fly in?" Molly asked as they neared it.

Rand looked up at the nose. Keeping one hand at Molly's waist he reached out to stroke the smooth metal with the other, almost as though he were touching it with a lover's caress. "No, this old girl saw action in Korea, but she's retired now." He looked down at Molly and smiled. "I hesitate to tell you the name of the plane I fly. It would give you even more ammunition than you already have."

She lifted an inquiring brow.

"Promise you won't say anything smart?"

"I promise."

He sighed. "An F-14 Tomcat."

Molly's laughter was a genuine peal of pleasure. Two other couples heading for the entrance smiled at them. "I won't say a word," Molly said, "not even how appropriate that is."

Giving her a hard, disciplinary kiss, he turned her toward the music and light. "Was," he corrected firmly.

Molly didn't ask what he meant.

The occasion for the formal party was a welcome to the new base commander, Captain J. Wilson King. A receiving line had been formed at the door.

"I hate these things," Rand muttered in Molly's ear as they waited.

Captain King was charming. Molly said all the right things, and soon they were free of the line.

The club was packed, but as they stood three steps

above the floor of the dining room Rand spotted a table for two in a dark corner near the back wall. "This way," he said, urging Molly forward.

"Oh, no, you don't, Ericksson!" said a voice off to their left. Rand groaned, Molly hesitated, and they lost their chance. They reached the table just a step behind the other couple.

"Come on, Pebbles. I saw it first," Rand complained.

Pebbles? Molly thought. She wasn't going to ask.

"But we were faster," said the other man with a victorious grin. "Tough luck, old buddy."

He turned to Molly, and when she got a good look at him she gaped in astonishment. Rand noticed.

"Shut your mouth, darling. He may look like Tom Selleck, but he's nothing but a marshmallow inside."

"Shut up, Rand, and introduce me to this gorgeous creature. If she's been in your company for more than five minutes, she must be desperate for a real man."

During the entire exchange the two men had been shaking hands and pounding each other on the back. Molly and the diminutive brunette with the Selleck look-alike exchanged hesitant smiles.

"When did you get here?" Pebbles asked Rand.

"I'm still on leave. Haven't checked in yet."

"Hey, guess who's here? . . ."

"How do you do," said the brunette, extending her hand to Molly. "I'm Candy King. Shall we sit down?"

Candy's smile was warm and friendly, and Molly, feeling rather out of her depth, responded to it immediately. She was surprised at the younger woman's poise. She looked no more than eighteen.

"I'm Molly Beddingfield. That's a good idea."

The two women took the only seats at the table. A

waiter materialized at their sides and they ordered drinks.

"Don't worry," Candy said. "They go off like this all the time. They probably were together at their last duty station a month ago, but you'd think they hadn't seen each other for years."

"You're familiar with the ritual, then?" Molly asked.

Candy nodded and grinned. "I'm a Navy brat. My father's the new base commander. Are you from around here?"

Molly nodded. "Virginia Beach."

"Great! Can you give me some shopping tips? That's a lovely dress. I need some things, but I'm just home for spring break and I'd rather spend my time on the beach."

Molly smiled at Candy's staccato speech. "I'd be glad to. You're in college, then?"

"Medical school." Candy made a face. "Second year."

"That's quite an accomplishment."

" 'For one so young.' " Candy finished the thought with a wry smile. Evidently she'd heard it all before. "I'm twenty-three. I know I don't look it."

They suddenly became aware of the silence behind them. Candy swiveled in her seat. "Hi. Finally come up for air, fellows? Find yourselves some chairs. Molly, this is Mark Lowry, and, Commander Lowry, if you don't watch your manners you're going to completely scare her away from the military."

Mark took her hand. "I hope you'll forgive me, Molly, because that would be a disaster." His voice dropped to a suggestive purr.

Molly's eyes flew to Candy, but she was grinning. "If you fall for that line, Molly, I have no sympathy for you."

Rand was another matter, however. He insinuated his bulk smoothly between them. "Hands off, buddy," he warned in a pleasant undertone that left no margin for misunderstanding.

The introductions were completed and the men found chairs and pulled them over.

Candy and Mark were fun, their verbal sparring during dinner affectionate but with an undertone of something more. Molly wondered about their relationship. Mark seemed to be pulled into Candy's spell, but he was resisting, too, determined to treat her like a younger sister. Candy simply wore a satisfied smile.

The evening was a happy success, for Molly, anyway. She danced and laughed, even flirted a bit, and had a wonderful time. Rand, it seemed, had a different opinion. Every time another of his friends came over to be introduced and ask for a dance, his brow became darker. Finally he glared down a brave young lieutenant (junior grade) and got to his feet, hauling Molly up with him. "I believe it's my turn," he said sourly.

"Thank you, I'd love to dance."

"Sorry," he muttered as he turned her into his arms. "I didn't realize that I knew so many people here."

Molly forgave him his long face the moment their bodies brushed. He inhaled sharply and fitted her closer. "There," he murmured. "That's where you belong."

The music was soft and dreamy, something reminiscent of a moon under a warm summer sky, and she lost herself in the spell of the romantic ballad and the man who held her. His lips lingered at her temple, over the curve of her ear, disturbing the wisps of hair there until they tickled her cheek. Her fingers moved slightly over his hard shoulder, covered by the formal starched jacket. Her nostrils were filled with the scent of him, masculine and rugged. Altogether, she decided whimsically, it was as romantic to be swept off her feet by a hero from the skies as by one from the sea.

"Molly?" Rand said.

"Ummm?" She sighed and nestled closer.

"Darling, if you slither like that against me one more time, we are going to be terribly embarrassed before we get back to the table."

Her head popped up from its resting place under his chin. The two glasses of wine that she'd had during dinner must have had more of an effect on her than she'd thought. "Slither?" she repeated, marveling at the word. "Am I slithering?"

"Yes, you are, and I love it." The hand at the small of her back pressed her nearer, giving her proof of his words. "But if you don't want to find yourself flat on your back in the middle of the dance floor, we'd better sit down."

Molly laughed at the mental picture of the two of them writhing on the floor. "You'd probably never make captain if that happened. Slither. That has such a deliciously decadent sound, like something Cleopatra might have done to Mark Antony. Do you think she slithered?"

"Oh, Lord. You've had too much wine."

"I certainly have not," she told him, careful to form the words around her rather dizzy smile. "Can you swim?"

He looked at her impassively. "You lost me."

"I believe that I could slither even better if we were in the water, naked."

"Molly Beddingfield!" Surprised laughter and frustration almost choked him.

"Besides, if I'm tipsy, it's from you, not the wine."

Rand halted in his steps, causing Molly to stumble. His arms tightened. One of her thighs slid between his for balance. Whatever the intoxicant was, he knew he shouldn't take advantage of her in this state. He really shouldn't. She would kill him in the morning. "Darling . . ." he began huskily.

Her laughter faded. "Yes, Rand?" She turned the full power of those smoky eyes on him with a hunger as intense as his own. Her lips were moist and slightly parted, and when his gaze fixed on them he felt boneless. Where her breasts were crushed against his chest he was scorched by the heat. But, strangely, at the same time his feelings were touched with tenderness for this beautiful woman.

Then she moved against him and the tenderness was relegated to the back of his mind, temporarily shouldered aside by a desire that threatened to burst its bounds. Lord, he wanted her! But where? Frustrated, he gave a defeated sigh. He was going to have to find a place to live, and quickly.

It was after one A.M. when the band played "Good night, Sweetheart." Molly and Candy exchanged telephone numbers before they left the club, and made a date to have lunch the following week.

"That was fun," Molly murmured sleepily to Rand as she laid her head on the banister rail. Her body swayed back and forth. "I like your friends."

Rand laughed softly. He was overcome with a wave of affection, watching her. "Obviously they liked you too. Are you sure you can make it up the stairs?"

She yawned, patting her mouth with a feminine little gesture. Her eyes sparkled silver. "I think so, but you'd better stay here for a minute to catch me if I fall."

He stayed far more than a minute, his eyes riveted to the darkness at the top of the stairs long after she had waved her fingers and disappeared into her room. His thoughts were whirling with the realization that he had fallen totally and irrevocably in love with Molly Beddingfield.

Six

"The house needs work, Molly, so I don't want you to judge it too quickly." Rand fitted a key in the lock of the faded panel door and stood aside for her to enter.

Molly hid a smile. This was a side of Rand she hadn't seen before. He had picked her up at the museum, refusing to satisfy her curiosity until they turned off on Eighty-sixth Street toward Oceanfront. He was as excited as a kid with a new gizmo. What was the old saying about a grown man's toys?

"Rand, I've seen houses that needed . . . work . . . before . . ." Catching hold of the door to hold herself erect, she let her voice trail off. She stood at the entrance to a huge room and stared unbelievingly at the chaos within.

"Come on. It won't bite." Rand laughingly urged her forward with a hand at her back. "At least not now. Your ex-boyfriend, Lee Hayward, swore he had the exterminator in last week."

Rand had thoroughly enjoyed his meeting with the agent. He had enjoyed the curiosity of the other man, and most of all he'd enjoyed satisfying that curiosity by making his feelings for Molly more than clear.

Molly gritted her teeth as she looked around, thinking that Lee had done this deliberately, a small revenge. He might think it funny to show a house in such awful condition, but she didn't appreciate his brand of humor.

In one corner of the living room, trash had been swept together, forming an odiferous pile, including beer cans, papers, and fast-food wrappers, that climbed halfway up the wall, and it threatened to topple into the middle of the floor. Someone had obviously found an unauthorized haven in the empty house. In another corner a large piece of the ceiling dangled halfway to the floor.

"The pipes froze and broke this past winter," Rand explained, following her gaze. "But they've been repaired since then."

Molly nodded speechlessly and continued her study of the room.

What might be hardwood floors were invisible under what could not even charitably be termed dust. Dirt was the only name for the smeared muck. She took a step, inadvertently lifting her foot out of her high-heeled pump when it stuck to something. She hopped about on one foot until Rand could grab her arm and restore her shoe to its rightful place.

Several panes were missing in the windows flanking the fireplace at the side of the room—

someone had taped pages from a magazine of erotica over them—and the huge sheet of glass that gave a view of the ocean had a long diagonal crack across its surface. On the opposite wall, bookcases rose from the floor to the ceiling and were crowned with beautiful carved molding, but someone had used the shelves for firewood.

She didn't know what to say. "It's very—"

"Come see the dining room." Rand led her through an arched opening.

The condition of this room wasn't as bad as that of the living room, but the ceiling here had also suffered water damage.

Molly shook her head sadly and put her fists on her hips as she faced him. "Rand, do you realize that it will take major reconstruction and a lot of time just to make this place habitable?"

"Naw, not really," he drawled, grinning. "It's structurally sound. I had that checked. The rest is cosmetic. Don't you like it, Molly? Doesn't it have all kinds of character?"

"Who on earth *lived* here?" She pulled a handkerchief out of her suit pocket and wiped her hands.

"The house has been empty for a year. Obviously, derelicts set up housekeeping," Rand admitted wryly, and smiled. "They didn't take such good care of the place, did they?"

She rolled her eyes.

"Give me a week, Molly. One week and you won't know the place." He settled his hands on his jean-clad hips and gave a sigh of satisfaction. "Do you know that this is the first home I've had since I joined the Navy?"

"Do you mean you've already bought this place?"

"Well, actually I've rented it, with an option to buy. I like it."

"If you like it . . ." She let a wave of her hand finish the sentence.

Rand wrapped his arms around her and lifted her off the floor. "You're going to like it, too, honey." He swung her around exuberantly and planted a hard kiss on her pained smile. "Just wait until I get it fixed up, painted. I have a crew of men ready to start early tomorrow morning."

"You have been busy today."

Releasing her, he reached for her hand. "Let me show you the rest of the place."

"The rest of the place" was as bad as what she'd already seen, but Molly held her tongue. She fully intended to give Lee Hayward a piece of her mind the next time she saw him.

"What do you think?" Rand asked when they had finished their tour.

"You don't want to know."

His face fell, and she regretted the quick answer. "I'm sorry, Rand. I shouldn't have said that, but my opinion doesn't matter anyway."

"What the hell are you talking about?" he demanded. "Of course your opinion matters. This place is for us."

"Us?"

"As in 'you and me.'"

Warily Molly met his gaze. "Could you be a little more specific? I'm sure I'll be here occasionally. . . ."

Rand took a long breath. From the first moment he'd seen the house he'd pictured them together in it, at least when they weren't stationed somewhere else. This tour of duty at Oceana would be for at least eighteen months. He wasn't that far from early retirement, eight years or so, and he knew Molly would eventually want to come back here to live. Now he had to remind himself to slow down, take it one step at a time, let her get used to the idea.

"Well, I don't expect our relationship to end next week when I report for duty," he said with forced heartiness. Then his voice dropped an octave. "I love you, Molly."

She stared at him, then turned away, putting a hand to her forehead, trying to gather her distracted thoughts. He was talking as if he expected their relationship to be a permanent one, and she had never given him reason to think such an impossible thing. Finally she swung back, her expression determined but her tone gentle.

"Rand, you're going too fast. I realize that I'm changing . . . have changed since I met you. You've helped me see how narrow my life was and that I needed to loosen up." She raked a hand through her hair and shook her head helplessly. "I'm very grateful to you for that. But love? I just don't know."

Hell! Rand swore silently. He felt like a bungling idiot, heavy-handed and awkward, the same way he'd feel handling one of those "willy victors," the huge superconstellation aircraft of the fifties, after twelve years of flying F14 jet fighters. He shouldn't have sprung it on her like this.

But for the first time in his life—well, actually the second, but he had been little more than a boy, before—he'd left himself open and vulnerable to a woman. And he was being as clumsy about it now as he'd been when he was eighteen. The fact made him furious with himself, and miserable. "I love you, Molly," he said again, very quietly. "Shall we leave it at that?"

Molly couldn't leave it. This Viking from the sea actually loved her, and she was hurting with the knowledge that she could cause him pain. She gripped her hands together at her waist, unable to control her turbulent emotions. She'd never expected love to enter into this relationship. Well, not as a practical issue, anyway. Romance, yes. This was to be a daring, enchanting adventure. A fantasy lived out. Not love.

"Please try to understand," she said. "I have a lot of responsibilities, Rand. Aunt Jo—"

"What about her?" he demanded.

Was he being deliberately obtuse? she wondered. How dare he put her into this kind of position? He knew—she had told him that day on the beach—no commitment, no ties. Molly's anger rose to meet his. "I can't leave her. I can't leave a seventy-seven-year-old woman to go traipsing off across the world with you."

Rand's eyes narrowed dangerously. The word "marriage" hadn't entered into the conversation. He started to make some sort of callous denial to save his pride, then realized how dishonest that would be. Marriage was what he meant, even if only by implication. "Traipsing?" he said softly. "You make it sound like some kind of holiday."

"To leave the family that I already have," she argued. "To walk away from my obligations. I can't.

We discussed this before, Rand. I told you then—no commitments, no ties."

He took her shoulders in his big hands and gave her a slight shake. "What about your obligation to yourself? To me? Dammit! I love you, Molly!"

She caught her breath, the determination flowing from her body, leaving her weakened. Her eyes stung painfully; the burning in her throat threatened to choke her. *And I think I love you*, she thought, but didn't say it. She should have known that love was what this was coming to, she should have seen. If only she could throw herself into his arms, forget the world of responsibility and duty. A weight descended across her shoulders, causing them to slump dejectedly. "Why can't we just go along the way we are, Rand? We can see each other, go out . . ." She lifted a hand in a vague gesture, intimating the rest.

He dropped his hands and straightened. "Sleep together?" he asked in a voice that rumbled like the threat of an avalanche.

"Well, yes." Her own voice was very small. "If you still want."

"Oh, I want. You know very well how much I want," he said heavily.

Even in the emotional moment she felt her lips quiver in sad amusement, unable to quite believe that this was the same Molly Beddingfield who had told him she wouldn't be the girl in this port.

Rand looked for a moment at her woebegone expression. Dammit, he thought. He'd like to take her over his knee. Instead he pulled her against him, wrapping his arms around her, burying his face in her hair. "Molly, Molly, love. What am I going to do with you?"

She swallowed the remaining tears and smiled into his neck. Maybe it was going to be all right after all. "Well, you're not going to do it until you get this place cleaned up, that's for sure."

She felt rather than heard his chuckle as he rocked her gently in his arms. "I'm not giving up on you, Molly."

"You may as well."

"No, you'll see."

"Rand, this is impossible." She was pleased to hear that her tone was surer, more certain, than she felt, as she pulled free of his arms. "I can't—won't leave Aunt Jo alone."

"Did Hayward ask you to marry him?" he asked in a low, dangerous voice.

The question came from out of the blue, startling her. "What difference does that make?"

"Did he?"

"That was different," she said flatly.

"How was it different, Molly? Because you didn't love him enough?"

"Lee was an idiot. He made it very clear that he didn't want to be saddled with an old woman."

"Is history repeating itself? How many times will you give up your own chances for happiness?" he pushed on. "How long will you wait? Until you're your aunt's age? Until the passion in you has died? How long, Molly?" His patience was ebbing now.

"Until I can make a commitment with a clear conscience!" she vowed heatedly.

"Is that all it is? Or maybe it goes deeper. I happen

to think we could come up with a solution that would satisfy everyone, but maybe you're using your aunt as an excuse. Maybe you're afraid of commitment for other reasons, Molly. What are they?"

He wasn't right, she told herself indignantly, he wasn't. She had always assumed that someday in the future she would meet someone, fall in love, marry. All men were not like Lee. But the future denoted some vague time, not now. Rand Eriksson could be on the other side of the world tomorrow. And expect her to be with him. She put her hands over her ears. "No! I won't listen to this anymore! I'm leaving."

"You don't have your car."

"I'll walk!" she said in her iciest voice, heading for the door.

Rand heaved a sigh and followed. When she would have stalked right by his car, he caught her elbow. "Get in," he said roughly, opening the door and giving her a definite shove. "I'll take you back to the museum."

Had she made a horrible mistake? Molly asked herself that question a hundred times during the nights that followed, and each morning when she dragged herself out of bed at dawn she was no closer to an answer.

Rand had not been around much since Monday, the day he'd shown her the house. He avoided being at the Beddingfields' during mealtimes and didn't come in until late every night. Aunt Jo didn't comment, except to explain that he'd called to apologize. He'd been working on his house, he'd told her, trying to get as much of the work done as possible before he had to report for active duty the following week.

The worst part of this whole situation, Molly thought on Friday morning, the day that Aunt Jo was to leave for Richmond, was that if her aunt found out about it, she would insist that Molly go with Rand. Molly wouldn't leave Aunt Jo to that loneliness.

She fixed two cups of coffee and climbed the stairs carrying a small tray. A soft knock on her aunt's bedroom door brought a cheerful "Come in."

Jo was dressed except for her shoes. She padded back and forth between her bureau and the bed, where an open suitcase rested. "Good morning! Ah, coffee. Thank you, dear."

Molly put one coffee cup within reach on the bedside table and settled into a chair with her own. "I thought I'd help you pack, but it looks like you're almost finished."

"Just about. Cornelia wants to get an early start. Her nephew is driving us. Did I tell you?" She folded a blouse and arranged it in the suitcase before tying the ribbons across her clothes. "And I've left the number of the hotel down by the telephone in the kitchen. We'll be staying at the Crown. Did I tell you that?"

"You always stay at the Crown, Aunt Jo," said Molly wryly.

Jo closed the suitcase with a snap. "Now, Molly, I want to talk to you before I leave." She picked up her cup and took a sip, then a breath, as though preparing herself for something unpleasant. "About you and Rand . . ."

Molly hid a smile in her cup. She was probably going to receive a lecture on the propriety of a single woman alone in a house with a man. "I promise I'll behave, Aunt Jo."

Jo sighed. "That's what I'm afraid of."

Molly almost dropped the cup.

"Marriage would be preferable, of course, but an affair between the two of you is better than nothing."

Molly's jaw dropped. She couldn't believe what she was hearing. "An affair?" she asked weakly.

"I'll have to admit that I don't know how young men think these days. In my time a man who had been paying such serious attention to a girl would naturally propose. If he didn't, her father would have been after him with a shotgun." Jo smiled, but the smile held a touch of tragic heartbreak that was impossible to miss. "It's quite obvious that you love him. If Rand doesn't ask you to marry him, Molly, I am urging you to take what you can get. And don't let anything stand in your way."

"You sound as though you're speaking from experience," Molly said carefully.

"I am. I'm about to tell you a story that no one knows, because it is such ancient history." She sat on the edge of the bed and fixed her niece with a serious look. "Too many years ago to count, Milton was in love with me. I was only sixteen, and my father thought I was much too young to even contemplate marriage. I foolishly listened to him rather than my heart and broke off with Milton. A year later he married my best friend." Her eyes looked beyond Molly, to somewhere in the unhappy past.

Molly was stunned at the information. She had

known Milton and Lucy York all her life, and he had seemed devoted to his wife. "Does, is, are you . . . ?"

Jo answered the questions that Molly couldn't articulate. "Milton loved Lucy. He was a wonderful husband. In fifty-eight years of marriage he was never unfaithful to her. Now that he's free he says his feelings haven't changed, but it's too late for us."

"Aunt Jo, it's never too late. If you love him."

"Love? I never stopped caring for him, but we'd look like two old fools at our age."

When Molly went back downstairs, Rand was waiting. Dressed in jeans that might have been tailor-made to fit his lean strength and a blue dress shirt with the sleeves rolled back, he was the epitome of masculinity. Her heart took a leap.

Leaning on the newel-post, he watched her descend with an unreadable expression in his blue eyes. "I have breakfast ready," he said.

She could smell the mouth-watering aroma of bacon. Rand had begun this daily ritual when he'd first moved in. Her aunt had demurred, but he'd been adamant, teasing her by saying that he had to contribute to the running of the household or he would feel like a kept man.

For the last three days, however, he had been up and out of the house before sunrise. Molly, and she suspected her aunt, too, had missed the warm comfort of their shared meals. "I thought you'd be gone by now," she said softly.

He pierced her with that stunning blue gaze. "Does Jo need help with her luggage?" he asked.

Before she could answer, her aunt spoke from the top of the steps. "Please, Rand. I only have the one case, but it weighs a ton. I always pack more than I need."

Molly watched as he took the steps two at a time. "Are you sure you're not skipping the country?" he joked when he hefted the suitcase.

"If I were, young man, I would expect you to keep this place going."

Molly groaned silently.

"Well, Jo, that would be a bit of a problem. You see, I'm moving out today too. Your niece will just have to fend for herself, I suppose. I have no doubt that she will do a wonderful job. She's quite a self-sufficient lady, you know." Molly wondered if she was the only one who heard the sarcasm in his voice.

"Moving out?" Jo asked blankly. "Your house isn't ready, is it? Why?"

"We wouldn't want to shock the neighbors, would we?" he said, answering the last question first. "Besides, the house is coming along."

"You're going to stay there?" Molly cursed her voice when it came out as a squeak. "It couldn't be livable yet!"

He shrugged. "I've stayed in worse places. We've accomplished a lot since Monday."

Breakfast was a subdued affair. Molly could tell that her aunt wasn't sure what to say, and she herself was trying to keep her mouth shut. She had one Saturday free each month. Tomorrow was it. Aunt Jo was going to Richmond. The opportunity was finally here for her and Rand to be alone for a whole weekend, and he was leaving. She wanted to scream in frustration.

She also didn't want to leave Rand and her aunt alone, but she had to go or she was going to be late for work. Where on earth were Cornelia and her nephew? If she left now, Molly was ninety-nine-percent sure Rand would receive the same advice that she had gotten upstairs. She couldn't let it happen. He would be certain to tell her aunt that he loved her, and she would lose her protection.

Protection? Molly questioned the word even as it popped into her brain. What or who did she think she needed protecting from?

Jo poured herself another cup of coffee and peered over the rim at Molly. "Hadn't you better leave, dear?" she asked sweetly.

"Yes," answered Molly, resigned. "The Admiral has called a meeting for this morning. I can't be late." She rose and kissed her aunt's cheek. "Have fun in Richmond. I'll see you Sunday night."

The day hadn't begun well, and it went downhill from there. By the time Molly climbed into her car at five, she had a raging headache, but instead of turning left, toward home, she made a right-hand turn, toward the North End and Rand's house. If his car was there she would stop. Her conscience wouldn't let him stay in that disaster of a house. It was silly. He could stay with her. They didn't have to see each other—if that was what he wanted.

Oh, Molly, be honest with yourself, she said silently. What you want is Rand, in the house, for the weekend. Unconsciously she smiled, the headache forgotten. She was discovering that she liked the changes in herself, liked them very much. And she decided that Alice would approve too.

The portrait in the upstairs hall of her aunt's house showed a delicate Philadelphia beauty in long skirts and a Gibson-girl hairstyle. But Molly knew from family tales about Alice that she was tougher than she looked. Molly had often wished that Alice had kept a diary. The story of the rescue was well documented, but Molly had always wondered what Alice's thoughts had been. How had she felt?

Had her family tried to stop her as she raced out the door of the Princess Anne and across the sand? She'd waded fearlessly into the raging surf, but how far? Up to her knees? Her waist? Those long skirts must have weighed a ton when they were wet. Was she ever afraid for her own life?

Molly sighed, glancing out the car window to her right. The sea was relatively calm today. Only a few clouds dotted the sky, and they floated hastily toward the horizon as though apologetic for marring the smooth azure dome.

Rand's car was in the same spot where he parked the day he brought her to see the house, but she almost missed it. Surrounded by trucks of every description, its hood ornament was the only visible sign of its presence.

As she hesitated, her toe nudging the brake pedal, two of the trucks pulled away. A man in paint-spattered coveralls called something to one of his cohorts, waved, and climbed into another.

Molly took his space. Only one truck remained, its sides slanted and caged to hold large sheets of glass. She turned off the motor and sat there for a minute, hoping that the last of the workmen would leave. She didn't want to confront Rand in front of an audience. This was going to be difficult enough for her.

Where was the man? Didn't he know it was after five? Plumbers and electricians and such never missed quitting time, didn't he know that? Finally she got out of the car. Nervously she smoothed her skirt and headed up the walk.

The sound of feminine laughter halted her knuckles a scant half inch from the paneled door. She hadn't considered the possibility that Rand had a woman here. Or that the knowledge would slice through her with such painful vengeance. She was biting her lower lip, trying to decide what to do, when the unmistakable echo of footsteps approaching the door warned that it was too late to do anything.

"I'll get it," said Rand, laughing over his shoulder. He didn't see Molly standing there until he had plowed right into her, shoulder first, like a lineman bent on protecting his quarterback. She would have landed in the wild growth of shrubbery behind her if he hadn't caught her with one hard arm around her waist. His laughter faded as his brows rose in surprise. "Molly! Sorry, I didn't see you. Are you all right?"

She regained her footing and straightened, pulling out of the circle of his embrace. "I'm fine," she said shortly. "I didn't mean to intrude. I can come back at a more convenient time if you're busy . . . if you have guests."

Rand didn't help her out at all. He was staring down at her with a mixture of dismay and wry amusement. Miss Beddingfield had returned, he thought.

But then he noticed that her hand was shaking slightly as she tucked a strand of hair behind her ear. He narrowed his eyes in puzzled speculation. Miss Beddingfield was nervous.

Suddenly a cartoon-style light went on in his brain. Silently he cursed himself for being so dense, so unseeing. In his supreme self-confidence he'd thought, because he loved her, he knew Molly Beddingfield in all her complex moods. He didn't. The realization came to him with blinding clarity that Miss Beddingfield herself was the result simply, the product solely, of simple nervousness.

Molly was at ease with him, but when she was unsure of herself, she fell back on the comfort and safety of her alter ego, Miss Beddingfield, who knew the right things to say, the proper way to behave, under any and all circumstances. Oh, Lord, how could he not have seen?

His heart melted toward his little love. The grim expression on his face softened to a tender smile. His hand went out to trace the curve of her cheek with his knuckles. "Hi, honey," he said softly.

Just as he had wished, her mouth relaxed into the sensual curve he loved. The expression in her eyes thawed, leaving them liquid and shining, the way he loved them. And the husky little catch was back in her voice. "Hi, Rand."

He dipped his head to taste her parted lips. "Through with work for the day?" he asked gently. Go slowly, he warned himself.

"Yes-s."

Refusing to release her gaze, he circled her slender shoulders with his arm. "We're almost through here too. Come in. I can't wait for you to see what we've done."

"Hey, Rand, hurry up with that putty," a woman's voice sang merrily.

Molly's gaze flew to the lovely young woman who was standing on a ladder at one side of the fireplace, her back to them. Rand knew what Molly was seeing. Long legs displayed to perfection in the briefest of shorts, a cool—and extravagantly revealing—tank top.

He felt Molly go rigid under the weight of his arm and decided to take a leaf from Miss Beddingfield's book. "Molly, I'd like you to meet Willy Fisher. Willy, this is Molly Beddingfield."

Willy turned her bright blond head to grin over her shoulder. "Hi," she said cheerfully.

"How do you do?" answered Molly with perfect politeness.

Silence. Rand slid his free hand into the back pocket of his jeans. "Willy is a glazier."

Molly looked at him with a stiff little smile and a slight lift of one brow that told him she had no idea what he was talking about.

His heart gave a leap. She was jealous. "She's replacing all the broken windowpanes," he explained, and felt her shoulders relax.

Willy descended the ladder and sauntered over to them. "Yes," she said. "I'm almost through here." She tilted her head and grinned up at Rand. "If I just had a bit more putty . . ."

Rand remembered his errand for the first time since he'd opened the door, to find Molly on the threshold. "I forgot, Willy. I'm sorry. I'll get it."

"No, no," said Willy, her lips curved in a knowing smile. "You show your lady around. It's my job, after all." She left the room in a lissome flow of long legs and bare shoulders.

"A glazier. How interesting," said Molly. She wondered how many glaziers Rand had called to find such a sexy one, and then chided herself for being a jealous fool. Rand was watching her closely. She didn't want to meet his eyes. She might find the same bone-melting expression there that she'd seen when he'd saved her from falling into the shrubbery. She forced a bright smile. "Well, do I get the tour or not?"

"Of course you do." The arm across her shoulders pulled her closer for a quick hug, then moved down. He took her hand instead and grinned devilishly. He was going to thoroughly enjoy making her eat her words. "You remember the living room, don't you, Miss Beddingfield?" he said as though he were prompting her to renew a forgotten acquaintance.

Her lips twitched in response, and she joined in the game. "Certainly. How are you, living room? It's nice to see you looking so well." And the room did. Even devoid of furniture and cluttered with carpentry tools, it was beautiful. All the broken shelves replaced, the bookcases glowed with the rich patina of fine wood. The broken moldings around the ceiling had been repaired except for one section, and the whole room had been painted a soft, creamy color. The most startling change, however, was the window facing the ocean. The indifferent sheet of plate glass had been replaced by a huge bay window, with storage benches built in underneath. It altered the entire character of the room. With padded cushions the open U area would invite relaxed contemplation of the sea and sand and saw grasses, which swayed at the whim of the breeze.

Molly could imagine a fire burning cheerfully in the grate, the shelves filled with leather-bound books, and, placed around the room, large overstuffed chairs, chosen for comfort rather than show. "Rand, I apologize. I don't know how you did it in such a short time, but this is beautiful."

He had not released her fingers, and now he gave them a firm squeeze and breathed out. "I'm really glad you like it, Molly."

She realized then how much her approval meant. He'd been waiting for it. She returned the squeeze of his fingers and faced him squarely, hoping, praying, he could read the mental message she was sending. Don't say anything, she begged silently. She wanted to enjoy today without having to worry about tomorrow.

"Would you like to see the kitchen?" he asked mildly.

Her relief was evident in her brilliant smile. "Well, a kitchen is not my favorite thing in the world, but if it goes with the tour . . ."

He laughed, relieving the tension in both of them. "Okay, I'll show you the master bedroom first. They're the only two rooms that are nearly complete."

"If those are my choices, the kitchen will do fine," she said, the prim words tempered by a saucy grin.

"To start with."

Molly didn't touch that remark.

Sunlight splashed through uncovered windows onto counters of blond butcher block, sparkled off shiny new appliances, and mellowed a gleaming maple table, set into another bay window, which would balance the one in the living room.

"I can't believe this," she said in wonder. "Furniture? When on earth did you find time to shop for furniture?" She was really stunned at the progress that had been made. How had he accomplished so much in only a few days?

"I called a store listed in the yellow pages and told them what I wanted."

"How resourceful," she said weakly. "And you had people working twenty-four-hour days to achieve all this." She waved a hand to indicate the whole house, not only the kitchen.

"Just about," he answered wryly. He looked around, then back at Molly, while he tried to decide about something. "Look, I'm really grubby. Why don't I go up and take a shower? You could defrost some steaks in the microwave, couldn't you? We'll break in the gas grill on the patio."

For the first time since she'd gotten there, she remembered the purpose of her visit. She lowered her gaze to her toes and laughed, but the sound was hollow and her voice was low, regretful. "I felt guilty about condemning you to stay here. I came to ask you to stay at our house until yours was finished, but you obviously don't need to do that."

"Hey." He tilted her chin up. "I need *you*, here with me. Will you stay?"

The shimmers down her spine were a direct reaction to the timbre of deep sincerity in his voice. The dryness of her lips was in response to his searching, roaming gaze. "For dinner?" she asked quietly.

"That's as good a place to start as any, I suppose. Will you, Molly?"

Knowing full well what she was accepting, she nodded. "Yes, I'll stay."

Seven

Why do lovers wish for a full moon? Molly wondered dreamily. The black velvet of a moonless night was so much more sensuous, since the mind had to rely on smell and touch. She and Rand were sitting in a dip between two dunes, she between his knees, wrapped in his arms, watching the scalloped phosphorous outline of the waves. He had swept her hair forward over her right shoulder, and now his cheek lay softly against hers as they stared into the darkness.

Their empty coffee mugs were anchored in the sand, but neither of them thought of disturbing the peace of the moment by going to the kitchen for a second cup. The silence had stretched comfortably for several long minutes. Underneath the peace and comfort, however, they were both aware of the anticipation in the air.

Slowly, ever so softly, Rand began to nuzzle her

temple, using his moustache to prickle her skin. The gentle abrasion awakened tiny synapses of awareness at each of her nerve endings, sending little messages to her libido. She turned her head slightly, touching her lips to the dimple that was half-hidden in his cheek. "Rand," she whispered against his skin. She closed her eyes and inhaled the scent of his aftershave. It was a scent she would always associate with him, bracing and spicy, seductive and masculine.

"Molly, love, you know how much I want you tonight," he murmured in the same smothered tone that the waves used to caress the shore.

She lifted her hand from where it rested on his forearm and touched his face, urging him with the most delicate pressure to look at her. "Yes, and I want you too. I want you to make love to me," she said assuredly.

He let his breath out in a rush, the only indication that he'd had it bottled up inside. Shadows were dense on their faces, but each searched, using whatever light was available from the stars, the eyes of the other.

Under the love and tenderness in his gaze Molly felt her faith—in him, in herself—grow, expand to fill her heart. Her voice was soft, quiet, but no less certain than when she spoke of desire. "Rand, I love you."

Suddenly, with her words, the sheathed charge that had been lying tranquilly in wait ripped through the fabric of darkness to illuminate . . . something. The space that surrounded them? Molly wondered if they saw from the electricity of high-voltage sexual tension, or with their hearts alone.

Whatever the source of the light, Rand must have

read Molly's absolute certainty about the rightness of this moment, because he moaned slightly as his lids fell. He rested his forehead heavily against hers. "I love you, too, my darling."

The fingers that lingered on his cheek urged him again, hungrily, in the direction of a kiss this time, but he resisted. His arms tightened, stilling her restless movements, and his breathing calmed only with a constraint that shook them both with its force. "Darling," he said hoarsely, "my control isn't at its peak. If I kiss you right now, we'll be making love on the sand in about thirty seconds."

With unspoken acquiescence and a bit of embarrassment at her own aggression, she dropped her hand.

"Give me a minute, love," he added. "I told you we'd set off sparks, didn't I?"

His eyes were still shut, so he missed the smile that curved her lips. "Hey, Commander," she chided with a shaky laugh. "There is only one question I have to ask you before we begin my long-overdue indoctrination."

The teasing statement had the effect she'd hoped for. He opened his eyes and looked down at her with a gentle warmth. He chuckled, relieving the almost unbearable tension. "I think I know the question, and the answer is yes. I will protect you," he said tenderly.

Her heart swelled at the loving promise. Her own lashes came down now to screen her expression. "Thank you," she whispered. "But that wasn't my question."

"It wasn't?"

"No, but I really do appreciate your thoughtfulness."

He laughed at her sober little thank you and raked a hand through her fiery hair, tilting her face up with a thumb under her chin. "Molly, my love, you sound like a bread-and-butter letter. What is the question, honey?"

"Does your fancy new house have a bed?"

Rand growled deep in his throat and covered her face with quick, playful kisses. His fingers in her hair moved restlessly, cradling her head in his big hand. "A bed . . . was the . . . first thing . . . I ordered," he said huskily, between breaths and kisses.

He rose in one smooth motion, bringing her up with him. She stumbled slightly, and the arm around her waist clamped her lower torso tightly to his. The heat from his body seemed to turn her flesh to liquid. He stood like that for a moment to get his balance, and Molly felt his hard arousal.

"You see what you do to me?" His voice was barely audible over the wind, now that they were above the protection of the dunes.

She looped her hands around his neck. "You do the same thing to me, but I . . ." Her chin dropped.

"You what, love?"

"I feel like such a—a *virgin!* I don't want to be clumsy," she said in a rush.

Rand nestled his face into the hair at her neck. She suspected it was to hide his laughter. "Neither do I, honey," he said after a moment. "I've never done this before either." His free hand scraped lightly down her side and back up. The heel rode the outer curve of her breast. "You must tell me what you like." He pressed lightly against her.

She caught her breath and pulled back to look up at him. "I like that," she whispered, wide-eyed.

His fingers swiveled to cover the soft mound. He squeezed gently, holding her gaze in the dim light. His mouth was curved upward, but he wasn't laughing.

Molly's lids fell. She was having a difficult time controlling her breathing, and if he hadn't been holding her hard against him she would have melted right into the sand.

His roaming hand found the buttons of her blouse. Her eyes opened again and she glanced around. "There's no one on the beach," he reassured her, guessing her unspoken thought. "No one at all, except us."

"No one in the world, except us," she said breathlessly, letting her fingers dip into the thick hair at the nape of his neck.

He had completed his task, and her blouse fell open to the waist. Still watching her face, he slid the back of his hand under the blouse, his knuckles seeking her nipple, already firm and ready for his touch.

She arched slightly, thrusting against his fingers. "Please, Rand. Let's go inside."

They weren't steady on their feet as they turned toward the house, and he kept his arm around her waist. How he managed she would never know, but her silk blouse was off before they reached the patio doors. He dropped it on a bush.

They had only taken two steps inside when her bra was tossed aside. Holding her shoulders, he turned her to face him, his eyes riveted to her bare breasts.

"Oh, Molly." He shuddered. "Unbutton my shirt, love. I'm aching to feel you against me."

Her numb fingers moved to obey without thought. When she spread the shirt open she was fascinated by the whorls of hair that covered him. Her nails scraped lightly, outlining the musculature of his chest. The slight abrasion against her palms was erotically exciting.

He pulled her forward until her breasts were crushed against him. "Oh, honey, that feels good."

Her breath escaped her lips in a tiny puff of air. Wrapping her in his arms, he moved her against him, provoking the most wonderful sensations. Stimulating, stirring, sharply pleasurable. Blindly, boldly, she came up on her toes to intensify the contact.

Feeling her response, Rand opened his mouth over hers, his tongue plunging hungrily inside. Her tongue met his willingly. He lifted her off her feet and took a step or two, then set her back down.

Her skirt landed on a sawhorse left by the carpenters, her panty hose on the newel-post. His deck shoes were kicked toward the front door. She wasn't sure where her shoes ended up. By the time they had mounted the steps, the only things remaining on them were his cut-off jeans and her earrings.

Sweeping her up into his arms, he strode to a door that stood ajar at the end of the hall. Molly nuzzled his chin, her lips teased by the jumping muscle in his jaw.

The bedroom was dark, and when Rand let her feet touch the floor he reached for a wall switch. A lamp spotlighted the bed with a startling whiteness that brought her sharply out of her dreamy reverie.

"Th-that's very bright," she stammered.

He grinned and swiveled the brass head until the light reflected off the ceiling. The grin faded as his eyes heated her body from her toes to her thighs, and the soft, dark triangle between them, from her stomach, across her rib cage, and over her breasts. "Sorry, I like to read in bed," he said distractedly, then added in a soft, almost spiritual whisper, "You are so beautiful."

Molly stood perfectly still, shyly proud that he found her pleasing, but nervous, too, under his intense scrutiny.

Finally his gaze reached her eyes. He noticed her agitation and brought her quickly into the security of his arms, giving her a warm, reassuring hug. "It's only me, loving you, darling."

He gently guided her to sit on the edge of the bed and knelt on one knee, to the side of her legs. The mattress was low, and their positions were equaled, their eyes on the same level. He lifted her hands, leaving a kiss on her knuckles, and drew them to his shoulders, smiling tenderly as he left them there.

His mouth slanted over hers, taking mock bites, wetting her lips in erotic play. Her eyes drifted shut. She stopped breathing, wanting only the taste of his mouth, the scent of him, the sensation of his hands as they found and caressed her breasts.

The slight hardness of his palms stimulated her flesh, until she swelled and her nipples pouted into his hands. His touch drifted like feathers to her stomach, drawing swirls on her skin, lighting tiny fires one by one. All the time his mouth was working its own magic, nipping, tasting, eating hers.

When one hand urged her thighs apart, asking for the freedom to stroke the tender skin inside, she thought she would go up in flames at his touch. But she discovered those fires were nothing compared to the conflagration that engulfed her as his talented fingers found her warm dampness. "You're burning me," she said hoarsely, tightening her grip on his shoulders to bring his body closer.

He resisted, teasing her with half-kisses. "I've been on fire since the moment I saw you, with the wind whipping that wild hair around your face, and your skirt around those beautiful legs. I wanted you even then."

"Then what are you waiting for?" she cried softly, falling back against the mattress, attempting to take him with her. He rose over her, shifting her hips until she was lying fully beneath his hovering body. Still he didn't let her feel his weight.

Instead his mouth followed the same paths his fingers had traced, exciting her to the point just before oblivion, until she was twisting helplessly beneath him.

Finally, after a breathless moment while he undressed, she felt his arousal at the threshold of her womanhood. Slowly, so slowly, he entered her. He was careful when she might have felt discomfort, but she didn't. Finally he filled her throbbingly, completely; expanding, extending, her universe. The feeling was piercingly sweet, like a hundred harps echoing in her ears, or was the sound the mewling that she made as she took him, swallowed him, closed around him, gently and tenderly, complete as a woman now for the first time?

She lifted her heavy lids to look up at Rand, wanting to share her exultation, but his eyes were closed, his control obviously strained by his overpowering desire. Elbows taking his weight, he was motionless except for the irregular rise and fall of his chest as he breathed raggedly. His face was flushed along the ridge of his cheekbones, and a film of perspiration glistened across his forehead.

"Rand?"

His eyes flew open, full of concern, and what she correctly interpreted as painful frustration. "Darling! Did I hurt you?"

She cradled his face between her palms. "No. And you can stop treating me like a virgin now. I want you to enjoy this too."

A sound like a strangled laugh burst out with his gasp. He let his chin drop, until his hair brushed her lips as he shook his head. "Molly, Molly." Then he raised his head again to pin her with his bright blue gaze. "You're really all right?"

She combed her fingers through his hair and pulled his face down so that his mouth was only a whisper away from hers. "Oh, I am *wonderful*." She moved her head from side to side, brushing his lips. "Or I will be, in a moment, I think." Her voice rose on the last word as he began to move inside her.

Their lips melded, hard and hungry. Rand's tongue slid into her mouth, caught hers in a sensual dance, matching its rhythm to the rhythm of his body.

Molly wanted to be a full participant in the glory, but she lost all pretension to rational thought as she clung to his shoulders. Her instinct took over, and she met his loving assault with a firm, upward movement of her hips.

He led her to delights that before she could only have dreamed. The journey traversed secret valleys and shining ridges, before reaching up toward the sky from the final brilliant peak. And then she was falling—no, flying, floating—as her body convulsed, split into a thousand shimmering bits, scattered and reformed to something as light as air, changed forever.

Rand stiffened above her, groaned an unintelligible word, and shuddered violently under her hands. He collapsed, fighting for breath against the tender, fragrant skin of her throat.

"Oh, my," Molly whispered when she could move her lips again. "Oh, my."

Rand rolled onto his side, a hand at the small of her back keeping them joined, her legs wrapped around him. "Molly!" He sighed, still fighting for breath, and hugged her. Then he drew back to look into her satiated, half-open eyes, hugged her again, and laughed jubilantly. "I want to shout and sing."

Molly laughed, too, but weakly. She felt that there wasn't a bone in her body that was solid. "It's only your Viking ego coming out."

"I know." He met her nose to nose and grinned like a little boy who's just made Eagle Scout. "Do you realize how fantastic that was? No. Of course you don't. You've never done it before."

"Neither have you," she reminded him.

"I know. I feel like some crazy damned conquering hero. But it was you, my sexy little love, my inspiration, who provided the motivation."

He was thoroughly enjoying taking his bows. "Thank you, sir." She gave a mental curtsy and giggled.

Suddenly he was sober. His lips branded her forehead. "My woman."

"Now, wait a minute, you chauvinist—"

"Do you think you're ready for a repeat performance?" he interrupted.

"Now?" she squeaked.

"Now," her young, carefree jarl pronounced.

The sun was creeping up, half of the red ball split by the horizon line, when Molly opened one eye. She immediately closed it against the glare. She hadn't realized that the room had such a spectacular view, but Rand hadn't gotten around to draperies yet.

She turned inside the warm arm that held her, until she was on her back. A soft chuckle prompted her to open her eyes again. Rand was propped up on an elbow, smiling down at her. "You're awake," she said unnecessarily.

"Um-m. Watching the sunrise. Thinking deep thoughts."

"Too early for deep thoughts." They were both speaking in whispers. Molly turned her head on the pillow to look again toward the sea. "It is beautiful," she agreed, and turned back, smiling sleepily.

Her met her smile, watching her tenderly and carefully for a minute. He seemed to come to some kind of decision, and she raised an inquiring brow. "Something?"

He kissed her lips, which were rosy and slightly

swollen from his enthusiastic lovemaking. "Why don't you sleep for a while longer? I'm going down to make coffee."

"Do you want me to come?"

He hesitated. "No. I'll bring you a cup when it's ready." He rolled away from her and rose.

She watched him walk, surprised that she was totally at ease with his nudity. But then, why shouldn't she be? She had learned his body last night as completely as he had learned hers. She'd explored his muscular thighs, his lean hips, the spread of his chest into the strong sweep of his shoulders. She knew him very well indeed.

He crossed the room to the closet and took out a robe, slipped it on, and belted it around his waist. It came down to the middle of his thigh.

All at once his silence began to worry her. She lifted herself onto her elbows. "Rand, is something wrong?" she asked quietly as he headed for the door.

He turned back to her, thinking how the glorious fire of her hair rivaled the rising sun. The edge of the sheet skimmed the tips of her breasts precariously. How could he tell her right now that he thought he would die of the cold if her fire and warmth weren't beside him forever? She had made a conscious decision to give him her virginity and he had taken it, hoping that the experience would forge a bond between them that could not be broken. Well, it had worked, on one side anyway. He would never want another woman as he wanted and loved this one. But it had also put the fear of God into him.

In the hours before dawn, when the human spirit

is at its ebb, he'd asked Molly again for a commitment. She wouldn't give him one.

"Nothing," he murmured, and left the room.

Molly flopped back onto the pillow and stared at the ceiling. She knew very well what was wrong, but she hadn't the least idea how to cope with the problem.

He had finally put it into words, had asked her to marry him. The proposal had irritated her even more because he had offered it at a moment when she was most vulnerable. And he had chosen the time deliberately, he admitted that.

She had tried to make him understand. If he weren't in the Navy, she might possibly have said yes, despite the fact that marriage was a big step and they'd only known each other for two weeks. But she couldn't commit herself to a relationship that would take her away from Aunt Jo.

He'd demolished that argument with the surprising news that Milton was going to marry her aunt.

"You know more than I do, then," she'd said. "Aunt Jo said he hadn't asked her."

"He'll ask and she'll say yes, eventually. Bet on it," Rand had said with a certainty that had given Molly pause. They hadn't discussed it further. He seemed to be giving her time to digest the information.

What if Aunt Jo and Milton did decide to marry? Molly wondered now. Would they have a place in their lives for her? Then she scolded herself for being a weakling. She was a grown woman, she told herself. She'd make her own place.

With Rand? She felt suddenly a bit like a small child pushed out into a cold world where nothing was familiar. It was a ridiculous feeling. Twisting onto her stomach, she planted a fist in the pillow.

Responsibility to your aunt is your only reason for not marrying Rand, isn't it? a little voice prompted from the back of her mind.

Of course it is, she answered.

And there isn't another reason, another part of you that is afraid of marriage because of your sisters' many failures?

Madeline's only been married three times. And she's . . . well, Madeline.

What about Louise?

What about Louise? Louise isn't divorced. She's happy.

Ha! said the voice.

Just because she's married to a philanderer. She has her own interests and her children. She doesn't seem to care.

Just because the money's good doesn't make the job any easier, said the voice. And then there's Michelle, doomed to a barren life because of a stupid mistake.

Okay! Okay! Molly put her hands over her ears to shut out the voice. But it would not be muffled, because it was born of her own doubt.

Rand's mood had improved by the time he returned with their coffee. The tray also held orange juice, toast, and jelly.

"Breakfast in bed? What a treat!" Molly said, smiling brightly at him. She was determined to enjoy this weekend. Still, she admitted to herself that she also had to put the voice to rest. She had to face her doubts squarely and come to a rational decision.

"See how good the service is around here?" Rand said. He listened to himself with disgust. Dammit, he would not let this woman reduce him to begging. He'd never begged for anything in his life, and he wouldn't start now. She knew he loved her. She had heard his proposal. Now everything was up to her. He wouldn't ask again, wouldn't plead. He had his pride too.

Molly put a hand over his on the edge of the tray. She decided to take a stab at explaining. It wasn't fair to either of them not to. "Rand, I have some thinking to do. I do love you, but I need time."

"Okay," he answered, taking a swallow from his mug.

He could have been a little more enthusiastic, thought Molly crossly. She frowned. She couldn't see his eyes, but his offhanded shrug didn't make her any happier.

They shared the coffee and juice. She let him have the toast and jelly, except for one bite. He polished off the last piece and set the tray on the floor.

"Now for breakfast," he said as he reached for her.

She held him off for a minute, searching his eyes. The tenderness that she sought was there. She smiled with a great sense of relief. "Am I being childish?"

He picked up her hand from where it rested on his chest and kissed the palm. "I'll give you time to think, honey, but I'm warning you that I'll take every unfair advantage I can. I want you to stay with me until your aunt returns, all right?"

She barely hesitated. "Yes. All right. But I'll have to go home to get some clothes."

"You won't need any for a while. We'll go later," he growled. "Much later."

"You mean you're giving the carpenters a day off?"

He nuzzled her neck. "They'll start to work downstairs without me."

She combed her fingers through his thick hair and smiled above his head. "Do you think they will enjoy seeing the way we left our clothes arranged?"

Rand lifted his head, looking confused for a minute. Then he jerked upright, remembering. He grabbed his robe, and she heard his footsteps clambering down the stairs, almost at the same moment that she heard the sound of a noisy truck in the driveway.

Eight

Molly unlocked the door and entered the kitchen, with Rand right behind her. "Do you want something to drink while you wait?" she asked.

"Wait? I'm going to help."

She closed the door and pressed against the big hand at her waist. Raising herself on tiptoe, she kissed the square jaw. Rand liked to touch and be touched, and she was learning. "You can't help me pack."

Her fingers slid up to link loosely behind his neck as he completed the circle around her. "I can watch. Besides, I've never been upstairs in this house. I've never seen your room."

"Okay. But I have to shower and change out of this wrinkled suit." She made a face. "You may get bored."

His grin was more of a leer, as he released her. "I'll try to struggle through."

"This is our rogue's gallery," she said as she led the way up the stairs, past portraits of ancestors and family. "This is my great-grandmother Alice, the one who pulled your grandfather out of the sea."

Rand stopped to admire the picture, catching Molly's hand to bring her to a stop on the step above him. "She was lovely."

"She had red hair too."

His gaze left the portrait to fix on the smoke-clouded eyes of the flesh-and-blood redhead beside him. His thumb sought and found her pulse. He realized when she spoke that their thoughts were running parallel.

"All those years ago," she said. "If she hadn't been looking out the window of the hotel that day . . ."

"If she hadn't been a very brave lady . . ." He smiled whimsically. "I'd be willing to bet that my grandfather fell in love with her."

"And I'll bet she fell a little in love with him too," Molly said softly. "But she was engaged and he was younger." She sighed.

"Maybe our meeting was preordained. Maybe I'm another inheritance from your great-grandmother, like the cameo you wore the first night I came here. Did you wear it because of the connection?" He brought her hand up to leave an erotic kiss within her palm.

"No, I wore it to keep the dress together." Her voice was a whisper, muffled by the responses of her body to the sensual gesture.

He chuckled, the vibration adding a tingling echo to her already simmering senses. "Get packed. I have scruples about making love to you in this house, but they could easily be overcome in about ten seconds." He dropped her hand and helped her upstairs with a playful swat on her fanny.

"I'll hurry." She ran lightly up and disappeared into a room to the left.

Rand continued more slowly, his gaze wandering over the rest of the family's pictures. He had almost reached the top step when suddenly he froze.

He blinked, a terrible feeling of dread and fear engulfing him, sweeping away the tender, loving mood of a moment ago. Before him was a photograph of Molly and her three sisters, Michelle, Louise . . . and Madeline. He'd forgotten about Madeline. What would he say to Molly? His head began to swim and there was a roaring in his ears.

Molly suddenly came out of her bedroom. "I think I hear a car in the driveway. Who on earth can it be?" Oblivious to Rand's stunned expression she crossed the hall to her aunt's room, which looked out over the drive.

"Molly?" His voice was a hoarse croak.

"Oh, no," said Molly at the same time. She reappeared at the door to her aunt's room, turning her blue-gray eyes on him. "Rand, it's my sister. What'll I do?"

"Which sister?" he asked, reaching blindly for her hand. A terrible premonition seized him, and he shook his head to clear his thoughts. Fate could not be so unkind.

"Madeline. She lives in Baltimore, so what is she doing here on a Saturday morning?"

Yes, fate *could* be so unkind. "Don't answer the door," he said frantically. "Molly, please . . ."

Molly suddenly became aware of the conflict within him. "Rand, what on earth's the matter with you?" She looked at him as if he had lost his mind.

Rand knew for sure he had.

Then she understood. Her mouth curved in a warm smile and she reached out to stroke his cheek. He thought that with her sister here she wouldn't go home with him. "Darling, Madeline won't say a word about us. And she has her own key."

That was the first time she'd called him darling, Rand thought wildly. He'd waited for an endearment, ached for one, and now he wanted to howl. His fingers gripped hers. "Listen, honey . . ."

With a nervous little frown she glanced at the door at the foot of the stairs. "I only hope she hasn't left her husband again. If she has, she'll be hysterical, and it'll take forever to calm her down."

"Molly . . ." The door behind and below him slammed ominously. Rand squeezed his eyes shut. Too late.

Molly's gaze sought her sister over his shoulder. "Madeline, what a surprise."

"Molly!" The word came out as a wail before the flood of tears spilled from those gorgeous blue eyes, and Molly's heart sank. "Oh, damn," she muttered, pulling her hand from Rand's grip. "I'm sorry, darling," she added under her breath as she scooted past him to hurry down the steps.

Molly had played this scene too many times not to know what came next. Her footsteps faltered for only a second, however, and then she enfolded Madeline in her arms. "There, there." She patted her sister's shoulder consolingly, her lips twitching as she became aware of the awkward picture they must make—the tiny younger sister comforting the older, who had to bend way down to put her head on a comforting shoulder. Molly gave a rueful, helpless grin to Rand, who was slowly descending the stairs. On his face was an expression akin to horror. She couldn't blame him. Men hated scenes like this.

"Benjamin is such a beast!" bawled Madeline.

Molly groaned silently. Oh, no, not again. She loved her sister deeply, but Madeline had a propensity for marrying the wrong sort of man. All three of her husbands were absurdly jealous. Of course, Madeline was a bit of a flirt, but she didn't mean anything by it.

Molly patted on. "What's happened, Madeline?" She tried to keep the resentment she was feeling out of her voice. If Madeline picked up on that feeling she would go into her "nobody loves me" mood, and that one sometimes took days to straighten out.

"I only wanted to go to the poetry symposium in Jamaica," Madeline said between hiccups, "but he f-found out it was being h-held at the hotel with the nude beach, and—and he said such *awful* things to me!"

"Madeline, we have company. Can you try to control yourself, dear?"

"C-company?"

Here it comes, thought Rand, his heart plummeting to his toes as he stepped off the final stair. He tried to send Molly a message with his eyes, but she was too distracted to notice.

Madeline turned in Molly's arms.

"Madeline, I want you to meet—"

"Rand! Rand Eriksson!" screeched Madeline, and

pulled free of her sister's arms to launch herself at him. "Oh, Rand, darling!"

Molly watched in stunned amazement as her sister wound her arms around Rand's neck and held on to him as though he were her savior, her lifeline. The amazement turned to a scowl when Madeline planted a teary, but very thorough, kiss on the mouth of the man who, only a few hours ago, had proposed to *her*.

"Hello, Madeline," Rand said in a resigned voice. His weak smile faltered when he saw Molly's stony expression. The chill in the atmosphere was fast becoming solid ice. Helplessly he began to pat Madeline's shoulder, picking up where Molly had left off.

Madeline raised her beautiful, wet eyes to him. "It's so wonderful that you're here," she breathed. She turned in his arms to smile tragically at her sister, but Molly noticed that Madeline didn't relax her grip on Rand's shirt.

"It seems you two know each other," Molly said coolly in what was probably the understatement of the year.

"Years ago!" blurted Rand.

"But I've never forgotten you," Madeline told him softly. "You were so sweet."

Sweet? thought Molly. Sweet must rank right up there with cute.

Rand choked slightly, but it was Madeline who spoke, with complete sincerity. "If you'd planned this, Molly, you couldn't have picked anyone more perfect to be here for me."

He was blushing, Molly thought. He was actually blushing! What was going on? Or, more to the point, what had gone on? "Shall we go into the parlor and sit down?" she asked through gritted teeth.

"Yes!" Rand agreed instantly.

"Okay," whispered Madeline, always willing to follow the lead of an available male. She let him support her wilting body with a strong arm at her waist.

When they were seated—Molly on an uncompromisingly upright chair, Rand on one end of the love seat, with Madeline plastered against him—they looked at one another, not sure where to go next. Madeline seemed to be the only one who wasn't aware of the distinct hostility in the room. She cuddled closer to Rand's broad chest as though she had every right to be there.

For the first time in her life Molly felt a definite dislike for this sister whom she had always envied and admired. Madeline was too damned beautiful, that was what was wrong with her! she decided. She let her anger feed on itself, vaguely conscious that when her anger subsided, when her emotions took over, there was going to be pain. A lot of pain. As she sat there, looking at her sister wrapped in the arms of the man she loved, she searched for something to say, something to do. "Well . . ." Brilliant, Molly. "How about a cup of tea?"

"Tea?" said Rand, clearly abashed.

"Tea?" said Madeline.

Molly shrugged. "The English like it. They seem to think it's a panacea for everything." She stood up.

"Yes," Rand said. "That's a good idea. Tea. I'll help you fix it." He started to rise, but couldn't seem to extricate himself from Madeline's clinging tendrils.

"Molly can fix it," she said heedlessly. "Stay with me, Rand. We have so much catching up to do."

"You certainly do," Molly muttered.

Rand finally managed to free himself. "We don't want your sister waiting on us," he said firmly.

Madeline looked at him as though he'd said something wonderful. "Of course we don't. I'll help too."

"No!" he said abruptly. "No," he added more gently. "You stay here, Madeline, and try to pull yourself together. I'll be right back."

Madeline put one perfectly manicured hand to her cheek. "Oh, I must look a mess! Where's my bag?" She found it still hanging from her wrist and opened it to pull out a compact and lipstick, a tissue, and a big fat brush, the kind that usually comes with blusher. They left her to her repairs.

Molly lifted the kettle off the back of the stove. She usually drank instant coffee, but what the hell, she thought, there were surely tea bags around there someplace. She ignored the man who had followed her and now stood rocking slightly on his heels, his hands thrust into his pockets, watching her. She filled the kettle with water, managing to splash the front of her silk blouse liberally, and slammed it back on the burner. She searched through the cabinet until she found a dusty box of tea bags. With little regard for the fragility of the Beddingfield china, she took down three cups, the sugar bowl, and the cream pitcher, then filled the pitcher with skim milk. The milk's slightly lavender color made her want to throw up.

There was one shriveled lemon in the fruit bin of the refrigerator. She plunked it on the edge of the sink and viciously tore into it with a butcher knife, plopping the ragged pieces onto a cut-glass dish. She arranged everything on a tray, then added napkins. Sheer fury had kept her spine ramrod-straight, but, with nothing left to do, she suddenly slumped against the sink, blinking from the afternoon sunlight, which stirred tears in her eyes.

The warmth of his large body gave her scant warning before he touched her shoulders. "Honey," he said softly.

Her spine stiffened. "I don't think I want you to touch me right now."

"There is a perfectly reasonable explanation."

"I'm sure there is, but I'm not in the mood to hear it." The anger was beginning to slide out of her, and the void it left was filling with anguish and hurt, just as she had known it would. She resisted, but the picture of Rand—and her beautiful sister—embracing, kissing, making love . . .

"Molly, my love, it was thirteen years ago." He squeezed her shoulders lightly. "You were in elementary school."

She lifted her chin, staring blindly through the window over the sink, trying to rid her mind of the picture. "You don't understand," she said, almost choking on the words.

"Then make me understand. Turn around and look at me, darling. Talk to me."

She didn't turn. If she did she would melt into his arms, seeking solace, but he couldn't comfort this away. "I've always worshiped them all, Louise, Michelle, Mad-Madeline. They are blond and beautiful to a sister. Tall, graceful, elegant. I'm the odd woman out in the group, runt of the litter. Short and redheaded, serious and studious, where they are lighthearted and vivacious. I worshiped them," she said again, in a whisper. "But can you imagine what it was like growing up in their shadows? They were the homecoming queens. I won the academic medals." Once more Rand tried to turn her, but she resisted with a violent shrug. "Can't you understand? Can't you see?"

"I see that you're the blindest little fool God ever put on this earth!" He took a long breath and let it out slowly. "You can't go through your life wanting to be something you're not, Molly. Being intelligent is not a handicap. So you're not tall, you're not blond. I can't change your height or your hair color for you—I wouldn't if I could. I don't want you to be anyone except yourself."

"I've always come in fourth in a field of four," she argued stubbornly.

The statement made Rand furious. "Who with? Yourself?" he erupted. His own temper was fully ignited, and he clenched her shoulders, fighting not to shake her until her teeth rattled, as he forced the anger under control. A muscle in his jaw jumped.

Her response was too quick and spoken without thought. "I've worn their hand-me-down clothes all my life, but I'll be *damned* if I'll take a hand-me-down lover." The instant the words were out she wished them unsaid. But it was too late.

A long pain-filled silence seemed to gel the air surrounding them. "Damn you!" Rand said. "Is that what I am to you? A piece of used merchandise?" he demanded in a voice so low, so tormented, that she had to strain to hear.

She blanched, wondering how she could have said such a horrible thing to Rand. He dropped his hands from her shoulders, but still she didn't turn around. She was afraid to now.

"I have some advice for you, Molly Beddingfield. I doubt that you'll take it, but for what it's worth, you will listen!

"I suggest you get your own life in order. Stop feeling so damned sorry for yourself. Stop playing the martyr. You stayed home to take care of the aging maiden aunt like a good little girl." His voice grew stronger and more sarcastic. The words were delivered like a load of buckshot, and she winced under each one.

"Did you ever stop to think that your aunt might not *want* to be taken care of? Did you ever stop to think that maybe Jo is worried about leaving *you* on your own, but she's afraid to tell you so? That that is why she won't grab the chance for happiness and companionship with Milton?"

Molly whirled to face him then, and, despite his anger, Rand could have killed himself for putting that stricken look on her face. She was as white as the porcelain sink.

"No!" she cried. "Oh, no! She wouldn't be afraid to tell me anything. We're very close." She fought bravely to contain her tears, which dimmed her blue-gray eyes to a foggy color.

Rand ran his hand impatiently through his hair. "Hell, I didn't mean to tell you like this. I meant to . . . Molly, I'm sorry."

"Is that true?" she whispered.

He tried to pull her into his arms, but she fought him like a wildcat. "Is it?" she demanded harshly.

"Yes, but . . ."

Could she have been that blind? she asked herself. That selfish? Why hadn't Aunt Jo just told her? They'd always been able to talk about anything. "Oh, God, you're right. I am a fool. I'm a double fool."

"Honey . . ."

"Will you please leave me alone?" she asked in a flat, toneless voice.

His control suddenly snapped. "Lady, you've got it!" He released her with an abruptness that sent her staggering against the sink, and stalked to the back door. He turned to her once more, his anger rolling over her in waves. "Hell, yes, I'll leave you alone. You wouldn't want to soil those lily-white hands with the likes of me. I almost forgot I'm damaged goods as far as you're concerned. You might remember, though, that you've already been tainted. Very thoroughly, if I remember last night correctly."

She inhaled sharply.

"I'll leave you and your spacey sister to your tea!" He spat out the last word. "You might find that the water will boil faster if you turn on the gas under the kettle." He jerked the door open with a force that threatened to pull it off the hinges.

The silly criticism brought an unwilling quirk to her lips, but she couldn't speak. She simply stared, saucer-eyed and confused, her mixed feelings clear in her gaze.

Before he slammed the door behind him Rand had

one parting shot to deliver. "I won't be back, Molly," he told her with terrible finality.

The warning jolted her back to reality. He was gone. She looked blindly around the kitchen. Had she really called him a hand-me-down? she wondered as she scrubbed the tears from her cheeks. When had she begun to cry? *Oh, Rand, my love, did I really say that to you? Can you ever, ever forgive me or forget such a cruel statement?*

She heard the crunch of gravel and the screech of brakes. He was leaving, literally leaving her here to cope with two hysterical females, one of them being herself. She ran quickly to the door and flung it open, but it was too late. She watched the taillights of his car disappear around the corner.

A few minutes later Madeline came wandering in, looking as if she were groomed for the cover of *Vogue*. "Did I hear a car? Where's Rand?"

"He's gone," Molly informed her grimly as she shut the door and leaned against it, her shoulders slumped wearily.

"When will he be back?"

"I doubt that he will." Molly finally pulled herself upright and reached for a tissue from the box on the counter. She blew her nose noisily. "Go back into the living room, Madeline," she ordered. "I'll bring the tea in a minute. You and I have some talking to do."

Madeline eyed her sister warily. "If you don't mind, Molly, I'd rather have bourbon."

Nine

The sun came up the next morning, as it always does, no matter how many heart-aching souls despair of ever seeing it again, to find Molly lying on her bed staring at the ceiling. She had a blazing headache, and was hungry—she'd forgotten all about dinner—and incredibly weary. Her throat was sore, both from talking until she was blue in the face to her sister—amazing how stubborn a clinging vine could be—and from all the unaccustomed tears she'd shed afterward during the long hours of the night.

She laid a limp wrist across her eyes. Now she had one more thing to do before she would be free to lay her head back down and cry, or wallow in her misery, or sleep, or . . . whatever.

Telling herself that her mission wasn't going to get any easier no matter how long she put it off, she rolled off the bed and headed for the bathroom. She bent her aching head under the shower spray, hoping that it would help clear her vertigo. She had sampled the bourbon, too, although in smaller amounts than her oldest sister. Lord, Madeline could really put it away.

The thought of that one sister brought with it reminders of the others. She had finally decided, in the wee hours of the morning, that she was finished living in their shadows. Rand was right when he said she had to be her own person. What was strange about his observation was that she had thought she was. Now she realized that she'd only been deluding herself.

Fifteen minutes and the entire contents of the hot-water heater later she stepped out, feeling not one whit better, but a good deal more determined. She slathered scented lotion over her body, from toes to nose, and scattered a cloud of matching scented powder all over the bathroom floor.

Because of exhaustion or depression or both, her movements as she dried her hair were careless and haphazard, totally inconsistent with her normal habits. She brushed the shining red mass into a casual fall down her back.

On feet that felt as if they weighed a ton apiece, she walked to her closet. She leaned heavily against the door and stared at the contents for a while. Suddenly, energized by a burst of anger, she grabbed an armful of clothes, stepped back, and threw them on the floor. Then she took out another armful, and another, until everything she owned except the golden dress was crumpled in a huge pile. The childish display of temper made her feel better.

She debated wearing the dress, but dismissed it as too obvious. That it would be inappropriate didn't occur to her in her present state, just that it would be obvious. She raked through the clothes on the floor until she came up with a pair of denim jeans that had been castoffs of Michelle's. She rocked back on her heels and stared at them. Why she had kept them, she had no idea. She never wore jeans, for the simple reason that she had never found any of her sisters' that fit. She was suddenly glad that she hadn't thrown these away. What she needed today was a totally different look.

Without bothering with underwear, she slid the jeans over her hips. It took a show of strength and a seemingly impossible sucking in of her stomach to fasten them. And when she was done she caught hold of the bedpost, panting to catch her breath.

The legs puddled around her feet, but when she tried to bend over to roll them up she gasped, as the waistband bit into her flesh. Rounding the end of the bed with a shuffling gait, she fell across the mattress. "Contortion" wasn't the name for what she had to do to get the jeans rolled up. And getting to her feet afterward was a major accomplishment.

Now for a shirt, she thought. She rummaged through the pile again with a toe, then with much effort managed to kneel awkwardly on the floor. Nothing. She contemplated the mess in front of her. Struck with a sudden thought, she struggled up off her knees and went to her lingerie drawer. Again she had to rummage through until she found what she was looking for, a white eyelet camisole that had minute spaghetti straps and was threaded through with blue ribbons. Tiny pearl buttons fastened the bodice in the front, down past an elastic waist to the bottom of a brief peplum. It had been a whimsical gift from Aunt Jo one Christmas, and Molly had never worn it. Until now. She blinked, unable to believe that the proper Miss Beddingfield was about to leave the house on Sunday morning wearing a scrap of lingerie for a top. Somehow, though, it looked perfect for what she had in mind. Thank heavens April had arrived, bringing with it the warmth of spring in the South.

A few strokes of foundation, a brush of blusher, eye shadow in a soft blue-gray, an application of mascara, and she was ready for anything, she told herself as she slipped her feet into thin-strapped flat-heeled sandals.

The taxi drew up in front of Rand's house and stopped in the space between her own car and his. Molly paid the driver, added a huge tip, and got out. She rubbed her damp palms on the legs of her jeans and walked determinedly to the door. Recalling the way she had stood here two days ago in just the same way, if not the same attire, she prayed that her reception would be the same. She took a deep, steadying breath and rang the bell.

No one answered. Oh, no, she thought, he wasn't at home. She bit at her thumbnail. Then again, his car was here, along with hers.

Maybe he'd seen her and wasn't answering the door. Or, she thought more hopefully, maybe he was on the beach. She noticed a narrow space between the door and the jamb. Tentatively she put out an index finger and pushed.

The door swung silently on its hinges.

Rand sat slumped over the kitchen table, nursing a mug of black coffee and staring sightlessly at the ocean. He was numb. Totally and completely numb. He had been this way for hours. Or was it days? He didn't hurt, he wasn't in pain, he had no feelings at all. When Molly stepped through the door from the dining room, he regarded her with only mild interest.

His indifference unnerved her so totally for a minute that she began to quiver inside. She wasn't quite sure how to proceed, so she prayed first. Please, God, oh, please. "Hi, Rand," she said finally, wiping her hands on her jeans again.

He noticed her nervousness first. Somewhere in the back of his mind a renegade observation niggled to be free. He shrugged it off. "Good morning, Molly," he said politely. "Would you like some coffee?"

"I'd love some. Shall I?" she asked, indicating the automatic pot.

"Help yourself."

Her gaze was drawn to the dark smudges beneath his eyes, and she wanted to cry at the sight of the lines that bracketed his mouth. "Have you been jogging?" she asked.

He looked down at what he was wearing. Shorts, an old Virginia sweat shirt with the arms torn out, running shoes. He touched his forehead to find it wrapped in a rolled bandana, and wet with perspiration. He remembered trying to wipe the images of

Molly out of his mind running until he dropped. He remembered lying flat on the sand as the sun rose, gasping to relieve his tortured lungs. And he remembered getting to his feet to run again.

He sighed and ran a tired hand down over his face. "Yes, I ran for a while."

She laughed under her breath, but there was a small catch in her voice when she spoke, and her body gave a tense jerk when she turned. "The thrill of victory, the agony of the feet."

"What?"

"Running," she explained, silently cursing herself for the flip remark.

"Oh . . . yes," he murmured, his gaze fixed on her, seeing her clearly for the first time since she'd entered the room. She was looking different this morning, he thought as he watched her take a mug out of the cabinet. Her shoulders were bare and smooth and beautiful. When she picked up the coffeepot he frowned over the display of her sweetly rounded bottom in the tight jeans.

Molly didn't wear jeans, he remembered. And these were much too tight for her. He didn't like her going around in tight clothes. Well-l-l, to be honest, he liked it very much, but not for other people to see. And what was that other thing she had on? It looked like something a woman would go to bed in.

She turned back, and her breasts swayed slightly under the soft cotton fabric. She wasn't wearing a bra! he realized with shock. Molly Beddingfield was not wearing a bra. "Where the hell is your bra?" he demanded severely.

She raised her brows at his tone and sat in the

chair to his right. He noticed that her movements were stiff. "I didn't wear one."

"Obviously. How did you get here?"

"Taxi." She sipped her coffee, set the mug on the table, then took a long, deep, body-straightening breath and plunged in to the icy water. "I don't have on any other underwear either," she told him mildly, watching her hands curve around the sides of her mug.

There was a long, black silence while Molly waited for him to comment. When it became evident that he wasn't going to and the silence had stretched to a screaming point, she ventured a look at him.

She hoped she would never see such an expression in another living being's eyes again.

Rand's numbness had been swept away on a tide of sudden, overwhelming, gut-wrenching anguish. He clenched his fist and brought it down on the table with a violence that jolted both mugs and sent coffee sloshing over the rims. "I never loved her," he said harshly. "She was a gay divorcee and I was nineteen years old, for God's sake. She was lonely and beautiful and I was enthralled, not in love. It was a craziness, a teenaged fascination for an older woman, Molly." The words spewed out of him, tumbling over one another. He half rose out of his chair and fixed her with a stare that held both anger and agony. "Are you going to punish us both for the rest of our lives because of a stupid adolescent infatuation?"

"No," she said immediately. Her limbs, frozen for a moment by the torment on his face, were coming back to life with a biting, stinging pain.

Her voice was quiet enough to halt his outpouring

and too quiet for him to believe he'd heard right. "What?"

She released her stranglehold on her mug. "I said no." Her voice was stronger, but it trembled slightly. "I made a mistake, too, a dreadful, shameful mistake, and I don't have the excuse of being an adolescent. Rand, I love you." She threw herself out of her chair and onto her knees beside him. Wrapping her arms tightly around his middle, she laid her cheek against his chest.

"Molly . . ."

She wouldn't let him finish. "And I want to spend the rest of my life with you, no matter where that may be. I thought I knew so well what was best for everybody. Aunt Jo . . ." She choked and threw back her head, blinking frantically. "Oh, hell. I've cried already. I don't want to cry again!"

With one swooping motion he scooped her up from the floor and onto his lap. His shaking arms contracted hard around her and his hand dove into her hair, his fingers spreading, bringing her head into the sheltering angle between his chin and shoulder. He lowered his own head and hunched his shoulders as though he could shield her from pain with his body. When he spoke again his voice was evidence of how shaken he felt. "Cry, my darling. Cry if you have to, but let them be tears of happiness, please. I love you so much, I can't stand to see you hurting."

She sobbed. She sobbed it all out against his neck, loving the feel of his hand protectively cradling her head, holding her close to him.

When the sobs finally lessened, he let her sit up straight.

"I didn't intend to cry," she said, sniffling.

He handed her a napkin to blow her nose and pushed her hair back from her temples with his hands, turning her face up so that he could see her eyes.

"I was coming over here to try to convince you in a sane and rational manner," she said, "that I'm not . . . wasn't fool enough . . ." She shook her head. "That you're the best thing that could ever happen to me, and I didn't, couldn't, let you get away."

The stammering, disjointed statement brought a tender smile to his mouth. "I love you very much, Molly Beddingfield. If I lived to be a thousand and told you every day it would never be enough."

Her soft, hiccupping laugh still held traces of hysteria. She mirrored his gesture, framing his face with her hands. He hadn't shaved, and his beard was abrasive in her palms. He smelled like a healthy male, his skin scented with outdoors and exercise. With her thumb she spread the moisture on his cheeks, touched his lips. "And I love you, Rand Eriksson. If I wrote it on every star in the universe it wouldn't be enough."

Their lips met tenderly, sweetly, the salute like a vow. But of course it wasn't enough either. Molly wound her arms around his neck, tightly. Her tongue tasted rich, warm coffee and the saltiness of her own tears, or were they his? The bright blue of his eyes darkened as she watched, and then with a soft moan he captured her mouth and hungrily devoured her lips.

His broad hands moved across her back. At their urging she arched against him, reveling in the sensation of his hard body so readily accommodating her softer curves.

Finally he broke off the kiss. He drew back to smile that half-smile that she would find sexy for as long as she lived. "I can hardly believe you're here," he whispered.

"Believe it," she assured him. "I'll be here—or wherever you are— forever."

He hesitated to mention the name, but the subject of her sister couldn't be avoided forever. It was better to put it behind them. "Madeline . . ."

Molly supposed that her sister's name on his lips would always cause her pain, no matter how much she rationalized that Rand was only nineteen years old, and no matter how many other women he'd made love to since then. "I convinced Madeline to go home to her husband. She left at dawn."

"You did?" He lifted a brow. "How on earth did you manage that?"

She gave his cheek a loving stroke. "Let's just say that I'm learning to protect what's mine."

He placed his lips on her forehead and asked quietly, "Am I yours?"

Her smile faded and her eyes grew wide and smoky-dark. When she tilted her head back to look up at him, he clutched a strand of her hair in a loose fist. He felt his heart pound, wildly, out of all control and rhythm, while he waited for her answer.

"I want to marry you, more than anything, if the offer is still open."

He closed his eyes with relief for a second, then opened them to chide her. "You should know, my love, that that offer could never be closed."

She shuddered, and his arms tightened. "But I wasn't sure. I said an awful, hurting thing to you. If you'd called me a hand-me-down lover, I might not be so forgiving."

It was an emotional moment that Rand knew needed to be tempered with humor. "Ah, but I might have been saddled with Madeline if you hadn't convinced her to go home. What a smart little wife I'm getting."

"And don't you forget it," Molly said with an unsteady laugh.

"I'll never forget it, my love." He studied her eyes. "It still hurts you, doesn't it?"

She tried to shield her expression by lowering her thick lashes, but he wouldn't permit it. "Open your eyes, Molly," he ordered gently.

She complied.

"I don't want you ever to hide anything from me, my darling. Don't you know that I share your pain?"

She felt a twinge like a tiny burn inside her chest. "Because you still have feelings for her?" she asked hesitantly.

He shook his head firmly. "Absolutely not. Because the knowledge hurts you. Don't you know that any hurt you feel is magnified tenfold in my heart, that I would have done anything in my power to spare you yesterday?"

She stared deep into his eyes. The twinge near her heart melted completely away under his straightforward gaze. "I think I understand," she finally said, very softly. "I love you."

"And I love you. Can we show each other? Now?"

"Please."

He laughed, stood up with her in his arms, and strode impatiently to the stairs. "Damn, I'll be glad when we get a sofa in the living room. Then we won't have so far to go when the urge to make love strikes us."

"Maybe we'd better put a sofa in every room," she teased.

He took the steps two at a time.

The king-sized bed was neatly made, just as she had left it yesterday. "You haven't been to bed," she said.

He let her feet touch the floor. "There wouldn't have been any point."

"I know what you mean. I stared at the ceiling all night."

He crushed her close. He parted his legs to bring her between his hard thighs. The scanty shorts were no hindrance to his arousal. "Never again, love, never again." Suddenly he pushed her away. "Lord, I forgot. I must smell like a men's locker room. I need a shower. You wait right here, honey."

She smiled as she sank to the edge of the mattress, thinking wryly that if it hadn't been there she would have gone all the way to the floor, so weak were her knees. "I'm not going anywhere."

He held her shoulders in a grip of iron and bent to leave a hard kiss on her parted lips. "This will be the fastest shower on record, I promise you."

Molly didn't time him, but it seemed that he was back in the blink of an eye. The water was still beaded on his muscular shoulders, running in rivulets down his broad, bare chest, following the arrow of hair pointing into the towel wrapped around his waist. She swallowed.

He used another towel to rub briskly over his head and face. When he emerged from under it, he looked at her with some surprise.

"You're still dressed," he said.

She tore her gaze away from the long column of his legs. "Yes, well, I may need some help."

Rand felt as though he'd shed years along with the sand and perspiration on his body. His heart took a leap of anticipation. "I'm always happy to be of service," he said huskily, his gaze tracing her curves with hungry desire. His body responded instantly, throbbing impatiently with his need. Forcing himself to go slowly, he crossed to the bed and sat, catching her hand along the way to pull her between his knees.

She put her hands on his shoulders for balance. "Thank you. These jeans are so tight they're killing me."

"Then we'll have to get you out of them as quickly as possible, won't we?" He reached for the snap and the zipper. The soft pop and whisper of metal against metal were the only sounds in the room, until he heard Molly sigh with relief.

He folded the sides of the jeans back and inhaled sharply at the sight of red lines on her beautiful skin. "Why on earth did you wear these things?" he asked as his lips sought to soothe the streaks. Across her waist his mouth moved, his tongue laved.

Molly caught her breath at the sensation. "I wanted to be . . . look totally different"—his tongue dipped into the soft hollow of her navel—"Rand!"

His hands slid the fabric down over her backside,

and remained there to stroke away the discomfort. She linked her fingers lightly at the nape of his neck, holding him close to her stomach, and bent her head over him, inhaling the scent of soap and male musk. She rubbed her cheek lightly against his hair and, using her toes, stripped off her sandals.

Rand disposed of her jeans quickly and tossed them aside. His arms clamped around her waist as he planted kisses across her bare midriff where her top had ridden up. As his gaze traveled up her body to meet her half-closed eyes, he thrilled to the sight of her unbound breasts under the soft material. His hands moved around to grip the sides of her hips, moving her back a couple of inches. "Would you do something for me?" he asked hoarsely.

She smiled, combing his hair with her fingers. "Anything," she responded without reservation.

"Would you unbutton that . . . thing you're wearing? I'm not sure I'm capable at the moment. And I very much would like to watch."

A delicious lethargy stole over her at his request, washing her with warmth and passion. Her lids drooped sensually until her eyes glittered silver from a narrow slit. Her fingers worried the top button for a breath-stealing second.

"Molly!" he groaned. "You're tormenting me."

Her sleepy eyes widened with devilish innocence. "Am I?" she murmured.

"Yes, you are, you sweet witch. And I love it. Would you like some torment of your own?"

"I don't know. Maybe *I* won't like it as much as you do," she lied, knowing that she would like anything at his hands.

"You'll love it, too, I promise. It will be exquisite torment, my love." But it wasn't his hands that he used. Words were his erotic weapons. He proceeded to tell her in voluptuous detail everything he planned to do to her when she got the top off, if she ever did.

Her fingers became thumbs, her knees turned to water, at the husky rasp of his low, mesmerizing voice. She swayed, her smooth, bare thighs coming in contact with his hair-roughened ones. "Rand Eriksson, if you don't stop, I may never get the darn thing off," she said dazedly.

His laughter came from deep within his chest, and he reached up to help. At last the final button was freed. The top hung open, revealing a strip of bare skin, and the teasing light in Rand's eyes disappeared. He lifted himself to strip away the towel, which hadn't offered much concealment anyway, and the skimpy top, which had offered too much, and lifted her by the waist to lay her across the mattress.

One of his knees was inserted between hers and he set about to do every single thing he'd promised.

Later they dozed. Molly woke first to thrill to the wonder of his arms around her, and the knowledge that they would always be there. If not literally—he was still in the Navy—then figuratively. He would hold her in a loving embrace for the rest of their lives. She tilted her head back from its resting place on his shoulder. The morning sun bathed Rand's features in its golden glow. With a loving finger she traced his profile, the broad forehead, the straight patrician nose, the strong upper lip and the sensual lower one, the solid chin. She continued down to his chest, bisecting its musculature, following the arrow of hair past his navel—

Suddenly she found herself flat on her back, her wrists pinned above her head. The light in his blue eyes was clear and guaranteed more delights to come. "I thought you were asleep," she said.

"The hell you did," he muttered as his mouth covered her willing lips.

"Rand, are Milton and Aunt Jo really going to get married?" Molly asked when his mouth was diverted to one upthrust breast.

"Mmm," he murmured against her flushed skin. "He wants to."

She twisted senuously, rubbing her leg along the inside of his, and he forgot to ask her why she'd wanted to know.

It was late in the afternoon, and they were sitting at the table in the kitchen, devouring cheese omelets, when he remembered the conversation. They had talked about everything else: When they would marry—next weekend, they'd decided—what she would do about her job when he was transferred. He'd been almost afraid to ask about that, but she'd admitted that she'd always wanted the leisure to write about maritime history full time.

Rand took a swallow of strong coffee. "What about Jo?" he asked finally.

Molly chewed a bite of toast thoroughly, her eyes brimming with mischief.

His mouth curved at the sight, as he remembered

the very poised, very stiff Miss Beddingfield of two weeks ago. His love had caused her to shed the mantle of propriety like a skin that was no longer needed. Her uninhibited lovemaking had surprised and excited him beyond imagining. He stretched out his hand and she put hers into it. His fingers closed tightly.

Molly swallowed the toast and, using her free hand, dabbed at her lips with her napkin. "Don't worry about her, she's going to marry Milton."

He pulled her up from her chair and onto his lap again. He had discovered that he very much enjoyed holding her this way. "And how do you know that for sure, my dear little seer? She hasn't said yes yet."

Molly's laugh was triumphant. "Because I am finally going to get my revenge on her."

"Revenge? On Jo?"

"Sure. I'll be the matchmaker this time. I'll drive her to distraction. She won't know what hit her." She chuckled gleefully and wound her arms around Rand's neck, covering his face with kisses.

He joined in the laughter.

"And," Molly finished huskily, "if she is a tenth as happy as I am this minute, my darling, she won't care."

THE EDITOR'S CORNER

We've received thousands of wonderful letters chockablock with delightful, helpful comments and excellent questions and—*help!*—there is no way I can respond personally. (I assure you, though, that I have read every single note and letter that has come in.) Here, then, I'll try to answer a few of the most frequently asked questions.

First, I must apologize most sincerely for apparently misleading you by asking the question about publishing more books each month. We have *no* plans to do so during 1986. Indeed, our publishing schedule is set for the rest of the year at four books per month, and I'm really sorry for raising the hopes of so many of you for more LOVESWEPTs.

Hundreds have asked for the addresses of favorite authors. We don't give out this information, but we do forward letters. It means a lot to an author (as it does to those of us on the LOVESWEPT staff) to know that you enjoy a book, so do write. Simply send your letter to the author in care of LOVESWEPT, Bantam Books, at the address below. We love playing Post Office!

Thank you for your generous comments about the author's autobiographical sketches and about the Editor's Corner. And, by popular request (demand, really), here are the coming attractions from LOVESWEPT for the next six months!

APRIL 1986
#135—STUBBORN CINDERELLA
　by *Eugenia Riley*
#137—TARNISHED ARMOR
　by *Peggy Webb*

#136—THE RANA LOOK
　by *Sandra Brown*
#138—THE EAGLE CATCHER
　by *Joan Elliott Pickart*

MAY 1986
#139—DELILAH'S WEAKNESS
　by *Kathleen Creighton*
#141—CRESCENDO
　by *Adrienne Staff and Sally Goldenbaum*

#140—FIRE IN THE RAIN
　by *Fayrene Preston*
#142—TROUBLE IN TRIPLICATE
　by *Barbara Boswell*

(continued)

JUNE 1986
#143—DONOVAN'S ANGEL
    by *Peggy Webb*
#145—ALL IS FAIR
    by *Linda Cajio*

#144—WILD BLUE YONDER
    by *Millie Grey*
#146—JOURNEY'S END
    by *Joan Elliott Pickart*

JULY 1986
#147—ONCE IN LOVE WITH AMY
    by *Nancy Holder*
#149—TIME AFTER TIME
    by *Kay Hooper*

#148—ALWAYS
    by *Iris Johansen*
#150—HOT TAMALES
    by *Sara Orwig*

AUGUST 1986
#151—CHAR'S WEBB
    by *Kathleen Downes*
#153—MISTER LONELYHEARTS
    by *Joan Elliott Pickart*

#152—EVERLASTING
    by *Iris Johansen*
#154—22 INDIGO PLACE
    by *Sandra Brown*

SEPTEMBER 1986
#155—GLORY BOUND
    by *Billie Green*
#157—MONKEY BUSINESS
    by *Peggy Webb*

#156—NO WAY TO TREAT A
    LOVER
    by *Marie Michael*
#158—ALWAYS, AMBER
    by *Barbara Boswell*

For this peek into the future we pay the price of very brief comments about next month's romances. Alas!

In **STUBBORN CINDERELLA** (isn't that a terrific title?) by Eugenia Riley, two extremely winning people meet in the most unlikely romantic spot—the supermarket—and it's spontaneous combustion from the start! But, heroine Tracy has only just begun to assert her independence and isn't ready to settle down. Only a Prince Charming of a hero like Anthony Delano could divert this stubborn lady from her plan . . . and you'll relish the way he goes about it.

THE RANA LOOK by Sandra Brown certainly will catch your eye on the racks next month! You'll see Sandra herself as heroine Rana and McLean Stevenson, host of the afternoon television program AMERICA, as hero Trent. The behind-the-scenes story for those of you who missed the broadcast last October, is that Sandra was flown to Los Angeles to appear on

(continued)

the program and show how a cover for a LOVESWEPT is conceived and executed. McLean really wanted to get into the character for the photographic session that leads to the final (painted) cover art. Sandra's advice to him? "Just remember that my hero Trent Gamblin is a quarterback and is used to calling all the plays . . . on *and off* the field!" She reports that McLean's sense of humor nearly got the better of her during their "clench" for this cover. By the way, the story is the sort of shimmeringly sensual and heart-warming romance you've come to expect from Sandra.

Peggy Webb gives us that most exciting sort of hero in her next LOVESWEPT—a knight in slightly **TARNISHED ARMOR**. Lance is a gorgeous male specimen who knocks prim and proper Miss Alice Spencer right off her feet. But he's also a ramblin' man while she's a homebody . . . and it seems that only a miracle can help them reconcile their differences!

Jace Dalton got his nickname—**THE EAGLE CATCHER**—from an American Indian comrade in the Air Force. But he needs more than the courage that admiring nickname indicates he's shown as a test pilot to win Heather Wade's trust . . . for she lost her young husband in a fiery crash. With courage and humor, Heather and Jace must battle a ghostly shadow to realize true and lasting love.

Again, thank you for your wonderful responses to our questionnaire!

Sincerely,

Carolyn Nichols

Carolyn Nichols
   Editor
LOVESWEPT
Bantam Books, Inc.
666 Fifth Avenue
New York, NY 10103